Łw

THE TYCOON'S INSTANT FAMILY

BY

CAROLINE ANDERSON

First published in Great Britain 2006
Large Print edition 2007
Harlequin Mills & Boon Limited,
Eton House, 18-24 Paradise Road,
Richmond, Surrey TW9 1SR

© Caroline Anderson 2006

ISBN-13: 978 0 263 19438 8
ISBN-10:   0 263 19438 8

Set in Times Roman 17 on 21 pt.
16-0307-45032

Printed and bound in Great Britain
by Antony Rowe Ltd, Chippenham, Wiltshire

PROLOGUE

'GIVE me one good reason why I should help you.'

The man sitting in front of him gave a tiny, helpless shrug. He was a proud man at the end of his rope, and it gave Nick no pleasure to push him, but he needed to get to the bottom of this request, and pussy-footing around wouldn't cut the mustard.

'Mr Broomfield?'

Another little shrug. 'I can't—I can't give you a reason. I don't even know why I'm here—'

'So why did you come to me?'

'Gerry told me to. Gerry Burrows—you helped him out last year.'

'I remember. We bought his company.'

'Oh, you did more than that. You saved his life. He was suicidal and his wife was on the point of leaving him, and you turned his life around.'

And this man looked in need of the same kind of rescue package. Nick shifted in his chair and wondered how many more desperate friends Gerry Burrows had. One at a time, he told himself wearily. Surely there couldn't be *that* many?

'Gerry Burrows had a business worth buying. As yet I know nothing about you or your business, or even what you want from me, so why don't you start there and tell me what exactly you have in mind?'

Andrew Broomfield's laugh was bitter and self-deprecating. 'I haven't even thought that far—'

'Then perhaps you should. If I'm going to help you, Mr Broomfield, I *need* a reason.'

'There *is* no good reason. Only a lunatic would consider it.' His laugh cracked in the middle. 'We buy and sell bankrupt stock, of all things.

It was doing really well, but then we over-stretched ourselves, bought several shops so we could open retail outlets, and things went from bad to worse, really. They're all mortgaged to the hilt, and our only real asset is draining so much cash it's brought us to the brink. It was meant to save us, but it's taking us under. We can't go on—and if I can't find someone to intervene, then I guess the receivers will.'

'It might be the best thing.'

'No.' He closed his eyes, his head shaking slowly from side to side. 'For me, yes, it's what I deserve, but my wife's pregnant, and we've just been told the baby's got something wrong with him and he'll need a whole series of op-erations, starting as soon as he's born. She has no idea the business is in trouble, and I can't do that to her—make her homeless just before the baby's born, with all we've got to face there, but I just can't see any way out of it—'

Oh, hell. He'd just hit on the one thing calculated to get to Nick, but curiously it didn't look calculated. It looked as if it came from the heart.

'Homeless?' he prompted.

Broomfield nodded miserably. 'I put the house up as security, like an idiot. It's nothing special—just an ordinary little three-bedroomed detached house like millions of others and a drop in the ocean compared to our other debts, but it's home, and I can't take that away from her—'

Nick sat back, twiddling a pen in his finger-tips and watching the man struggle with his emotions. God, he was getting soft in his old age. He knew he was only going through the motions here, knew he'd help Broomfield even though he didn't know him from Adam and shouldn't care a jot about his pregnant wife or the sick baby or the mess he'd got them in.

He stuck to the facts. 'Tell me about this asset.'

The man shrugged again. 'It's just a building site—a tatty, near-derelict old school with a disused chapel and other bits and pieces, and a handful of temporary classrooms scattered about the site. I bought it a few years ago and sat on it, and last year we got planning permission for conversion and a small development on the playing fields. We should have sold it then, but—well, I thought we'd make more if we developed it ourselves, but I underestimated the cost of the work. Drastically.'

'So you've started doing it.'

'Yes, but we've just run out of money. We put the builder on a penalty clause to move things along faster, but we can't afford to pay him and so everything's come to a grinding halt. I've bought us a little time, managed to stop him walking out, but only because we owe them so much they won't walk until they get their money.'

'How much are we talking about?' Nick asked.

'I'm not sure—thousands. Hundreds of thousands, probably.'

Nick nodded, wondering how he could have got into so much debt and not know the figure.

Presumably that was how. 'And the other debts, on your business?'

He shrugged again. 'The same—more, perhaps. The business is in real trouble, but if you knew what you were doing you might get something out of it, and if you could sell the shops they might almost clear the mortgage debt, but it would take time and that's one thing we haven't got. It's only really the site that's of significant value, and that's only potential. Frankly at the moment it's worth less than it was when we started.'

Nick's entrepreneurial antennae twitched. Potential was one of his favourite words, and another one was honesty. Nobody could accuse Broomfield of trying to cover anything up. He was being distressingly honest at his own expense, but for Nick, at least, it worked. To a point.

'OK. I'll try and find time to go and see the site when I get back from New York in a few days—and in the meantime I want exact figures on the business, the mortgages and the property portfolio. If they stack up, we'll talk again.'

'If I could just keep my house—'

'I'm not making any promises. I'm not in this for charity, Mr Broomfield—but I'll do what I can.'

'Do you *know* what you're buying?'

Nick shrugged off his jacket, dropped into the big leather chair behind his desk and studied the incredulous face of his PA for a moment before he sat back, twiddling his pen.

'Want to give me a clue what you're talking about?'

Tory sighed and plonked herself down in the chair opposite, rolling her eyes. 'The Broomfield deal—the building site?'

He scrunched his brows together, racking his brains and trying to dredge up something—anything!—that would have put that look on

Tory's face. 'What about it?' he said. 'Some scruffy old school buildings, he said. Nothing great. Potential, I think was the word—'

'Nothing great?' Tory snorted and waggled a fat manila folder at him. 'I take it you haven't looked at the plans I carefully faxed you?'

Nick grinned. 'Guilty as charged,' he confessed.

'I thought so. The *scruffy old school buildings* are a rather fine Victorian house in the style of an Italianate villa, with a coach house, chapel, stable block et cetera, et cetera, blah, blah, blah. With a couple of acres of playing fields. OK, there are some tatty old temporary classrooms and some other bits from the days when it was a school that need demolishing, but that's all and they may already have gone. The rest is a gem. For goodness' sake, it's prime real estate, on a seafront site in a prime residential area of Yoxburgh, in Suffolk. You might at least look a bit interested.'

He sat up straighter. He knew Yoxburgh—

he'd spent days there as a child, playing on the beach, and his mother lived only twenty or so miles from it now. 'You said plans,' he reminded Tory, eyeing the folder thoughtfully.

'Oh, yes. Detailed planning permission for conversion to apartments and town houses, and the erection of several more dwellings on the site. Nothing very inspired for the most part, but it's a gold mine, for all that, and it's about to be yours, if you've got any sense.'

A little flicker of something that might have been excitement stirred his senses. 'Do we know anything about the builder?'

'Yup—local contractor by the name of George Cauldwell. He's got an excellent reputation, apparently. I checked him out. Been in the business for years and I couldn't find a whiff of an unsatisfied customer. It should be an interesting little development if it's as successful as his others—and it could be worth a tidy fortune. Someone's been very, very sloppy—or they have no idea what they're sitting on.'

'Desperate, I think is the word.' He thought of Andrew Broomfield, living with his pregnant wife in a little house on the brink of repossession and with a medical crisis looming for the baby, and felt a sense of relief that maybe, just maybe, they'd come out of this smelling of roses. Sort of. Certainly from what he'd seen of the figures the business itself wouldn't be worth anything like what it would cost to clear the debts, so the building site had to be pretty fantastic to justify his altruistic gesture.

And if the look on Tory's face was anything to go by...

He gestured to the bulging folder. 'Are those the plans, by any chance?'

The folder arrived on his desk, skidding towards him and coming to a halt under his outstretched hand. He flicked through it, unfolding the plans and flattening them out on the desk, the significance of the deal finally sinking in as he scanned the drawings.

He ran his mind over the things he had to do today, the things he could delegate or leave until tomorrow, and refolded the plans, shuffling them back into the folder and getting to his feet. 'I'm going to have a look—see if I can get a feel for it.'

'Fine. I'll schedule a meeting—'

'No. I'm going now.'

'But you've got lunch booked with Simon Darcy—'

'You can handle it. Simon adores you—just don't let him talk you into going to work for him, that's all I ask. You don't need me there. I could do with some sea air. I'll be back later.'

'I'll phone them—tell the contractor that you're coming. They've been hounding Andrew Broomfield for money the whole time you were in New York and he's getting frantic for your answer. He's running out of lies to tell them, I think, and they're only a small firm. They'll be pleased to see you.'

'No. Don't warn them. I want to see how this George Cauldwell runs the site before I commit myself. I'd hate you to spoil my surprise.'

Tory opened her mouth, thought better of arguing and shut it again. 'Fine. Just leave your phone on.'

Not a chance. He'd suddenly realised how bored he was, how dull and repetitive and endless his working life had become. He'd been in New York closing another deal, and he'd had six hours' sleep in three days. He was tired, he was stifled, and he needed some down time.

And so now, today, just for a while, Nick Barron was slipping the leash.

CHAPTER ONE

IT WAS deathly quiet on the site.

Well, it would be, Georgie thought philosophically. She'd sent all the workmen home days ago, and if it wasn't for the fact that she couldn't sleep at night for worry, she wouldn't have been here either, but she had nothing else to do and she'd cleaned the house to within an inch of its life since her father had gone into hospital, so she'd come down to go over the figures—again!—to see if there was a magic trick or two she'd missed.

There wasn't.

She propped her head on her hands and sighed, staring out over the deserted site to the sea. No magic tricks, no way out, just the bank about to foreclose and her father's health in ruins.

Not to mention her dreams.

She stood up and pulled on her coat. Sitting here was achieving nothing. She might as well check the buildings, make sure there hadn't been any vandalism. She reached for the obligatory hard hat and wrinkled her nose. She hated the hat, but rules were rules.

Archie was at her heels, his stubby tail wriggling with enthusiasm, and his cheerful grin made her smile. 'Come on, then, little man. Let's go and check it all out.'

She shut the door of the site office, crossed the site in the biting March wind and unlocked the side door of the main house—the door that, without an unprecedented stroke of luck, would never now become her front door.

They climbed the stairs together, her footsteps echoing in the emptiness, Archie's toenails clattering on the wooden treads, and finally they emerged into the room at the top of the big square tower. It wasn't huge, but it was her eyrie, the room she'd hoped to have as her bedroom, with windows on three sides and the most stunning views over the bay and far out to sea.

It was also the best place to view the site, and she stared down over the mangled earth, the pegged-out footings, the half-finished coach-house conversions, the sanatorium as yet untouched, the chapel almost completely concealed by the trees that had grown up to surround it.

So much to do, so much potential—such a waste. Even if Broomfield came up with the money, the design was inherently flawed and horribly over-developed.

'In your opinion,' she reminded herself sternly. 'You aren't the only person in the world. Other people are allowed a say.'

Even if they had no vision, no imagination, no—no *soul,* dammit. She turned away in disgust, and her eye was caught by a lone figure standing on the edge of the lawn below the house, staring out over the sea.

'Who's that, Arch?' she murmured, and the dog, picking up on her sudden stillness, flew down the stairs and out of the door, racing off across the site, barking his head off.

Rats. The last thing—absolutely the last thing—Georgie needed this morning was a visitor. She'd got yet more phone calls to make, because unless she could screw some kind of sensible answer out of Andrew Broomfield by the end of the day, the bank was going to take them to the cleaners.

Big time.

And now, she realised, running down the stairs after the dog, she had some random stranger wandering around all over her site, un-invited and unannounced, and the place was a minefield. The last thing—the other last thing, in fact—that she needed at the moment was someone slapping a lawsuit on her because he'd tripped over a brick!

'Archie! Come here!' she yelled, but the wind caught her voice and anyway, Archie had better things to do. The little terrier was on his back, legs in the air, having the tummy-tickle of his life, and obedience wasn't remotely on his agenda. Knowing when she was beaten, she switched her attention to the man. Maybe she'd have more luck there.

'Excuse me!'

He straightened up, to Archie's disappointment, and turned towards her, his expression concealed by the wrap-around designer sunglasses shielding his eyes. They didn't hide the smile, though, and her heart did a crazy little flip-flop in response.

'Good morning.'

Oh, lord, his voice was like rough silk, and her heart skittered again.

'Morning.'

It was the only word she could manage. She took the last two strides across the mangled drive, scrambled up beside him on the lawn and tilted back her head, one hand clamped firmly on her hard hat.

He towered over her—not that that was hard. If only he'd been on the drive, she could have positioned herself above him on the lawn; even that slight advantage would have helped, she thought, but then he peeled off the sunglasses and she found herself staring up into eyes the colour of rain-washed slate, and her breath jammed in her throat.

No. Flat on his back he'd still have the advantage. There was just something about him, something very male and confident and self-assured that dried up her mouth and made her legs turn to jelly.

If he was a representative of the bank she was stuffed. The last man they'd sent from the bank had been small and mild and ineffectual and she'd managed to bamboozle him with one hand tied behind her back.

Not this one, in his soft, battered leather jacket and designer jeans, with his searching eyes and uncompromising jaw. This one was a real handful. Well, tough. So was she, and she had more riding on it. If he was from the bank, she'd take him by the scruff of the neck and show him exactly why they needed so much money—and he'd listen. She wouldn't give him a choice.

Anyway, he couldn't be all bad, because Archie was standing on his back legs, filthy front paws propped up on that expensively clad thigh, his tail going nineteen to the dozen as he licked furiously at the hand dangling conveniently in range, the fingers tickling him still.

There was a possibility, of course, that he could just be an idly curious member of the public. She straightened her shoulders, slapped her leg for the dog and sucked in a breath.

'Can I help you? Archie, come *here!*'

'I don't know yet. I was just having a look round—getting a feel for it.'

The tension eased, replaced instantly by irritation. The idly curious were the bane of her life, and this one was no exception. Even with those gorgeous eyes.

No. Forget the eyes. 'I'm sorry, you can't just look round without reporting to the site office,' she told him firmly. 'Archie, *here! Now!* There's a sign there forbidding people to walk about the site without authority. Visitors must report to the site office on the way in. You can't just crawl about all over it, it's dangerous—!'

'Don't tell me—you're the health and safety official,' he said, that beautifully sculptured mouth twitching with laughter, and she felt her brows climb with her temper.

'No—I'm the site agent, and I'm getting heartily sick of people wandering about on my site as if they own it! Why is it that everybody treats building sites as public open spaces?' she continued, warming up to her pet hate. 'This is private property, and if you refuse to follow procedures, I'll have no alternative but to ask you to leave—'

'That may be a little hasty,' he said softly.

'You think so?' She raked him with her eyes, then met that cool, steely blue gaze again with mounting anger. 'Well, I'm sorry, we don't need you suing us, so if you won't comply with site rules, you'll give me no choice but to ask you to leave my site before you hurt yourself.'

'*Your* site?' His voice was mocking, and she had to struggle with the urge to hit him.

'That's right,' she retorted, hanging on to her temper with difficulty. 'Mine. Now, are you going to do this the easy way, or am I going to call the police?'

His head shook slowly from side to side, and the smile which had long faded was replaced by a slow, simmering anger that more than matched her own. 'Oh, I'm going nowhere. You might be, though, and hopefully taking your dog with you before he licks me to death. Now, I'm going to have a look around, and while I do that, perhaps you'd be kind enough to tell George Cauldwell I'm looking for him. Although I'm beginning to think I may have very little to say to him. The name's Barron, by the way. Nick Barron.'

Uh-oh. The name meant nothing to her, but it was obviously supposed to and she was beginning to get a sinking feeling about this man. If he was looking for her father, then he might well be someone from the bank, although his jeans and leather jacket made that seem unlikely, but if not the bank, then who…?

'He's not here,' she told him. 'Are you from the bank?'

'Not exactly. Will he be back today?'

Not exactly? What did that mean? She shook her head. 'No. I'm his daughter,

Georgia,' she said warily. 'I'm in charge while he's—away.'

'In which case, since you claim to be in charge, perhaps you'll be good enough, in your father's absence, to give me a guided tour of the whole development. If I'm going to be foolish enough to proceed with the purchase, I want to see every last square inch. In triplicate.'

The purchase? The whole development?

Oh, lord, what had she *done?* This project was the biggest development her father had ever taken on, and standing in front of her was the man who had the power to make or break them. And she'd just threatened him with the police!

Fantastic. For the last two months they'd been throwing money into the site, forging ahead with the conversions and making a start on the new builds, and all the time waiting for instructions and—most importantly—funds. They'd been trying to get to the point of another stage payment, but all the way along they'd been delayed by a lack of detail in the specifications. Although Broomfield's company seemed big on ideas, they were miserably short on detail, and the devil, in this case, was certainly in the detail. With the clock running on the penalty clause, it was debatable whose fault it would be.

And now the man who could have been the answer to her prayers was right here in front of her, and if she hadn't already screwed up totally, she wasn't going to let him leave until she'd had a chance to put their side of it and hopefully secure his promise to clear their debts, at the very least.

But her first move had better be an apology— a good one. She forced herself to meet his eyes and her heart sank. He was clearly running out of patience, and his eyes were sceptical and filled with doubts—doubts she had to get rid of at all costs.

'I'm sorry, I hadn't been told anything about a buy-out,' she confessed. 'My father's been in hospital for nearly two weeks, and I've been dealing with Andrew Broomfield—or trying to. He's been avoiding me.'

'I wonder why?' he murmured.

She swallowed her pride. The first apology obviously hadn't worked. She'd have to try harder, and she forced herself to hold his eyes.

'Look, I'm sorry. I was really rude, I apologise. I'm not normally like this, but I thought you were just being nosy, so I took it out on you. We've had some vandalism and thefts on the site, so I'm a bit edgy when I'm here on my own—'

'I look like a vandal?'

No, she thought, you look like an avenging angel, and this is going from bad to worse. She shook her head, closing her eyes and wondering if he'd still be there when she opened them.

He was. Damn. She tried again. 'No, of course you don't, but it's been a rough day so far and I wasn't thinking. Can we start again?'

For a moment he just studied her, then his face softened almost imperceptibly. 'Sounds like it's been a rough month.'

She laughed a little hysterically. 'You could say that. Look, I'm really sorry. I had no idea you were taking it over, Andrew's been really cagey recently. Of course you can see the site, I'd be delighted to show you round, but I do need to get you kitted out with a hard hat and you need to sign in, and maybe while we do that I can answer some of your questions.'

'It sounds like you have more questions than I do.'

She gave a wry, slightly bitter laugh. 'Only one that matters, and I guess that'll have to wait. We're owed a stage payment, and the bank's beginning to get edgy. And I've just hit a brick wall with Andrew. Yesterday I got some garbled message about money in the pipeline, but nothing I can take to the bank.'

His lips tightened. 'That may be my fault.

I've been out of the country and I haven't given him an answer yet.'

'And I've done my best to put you off,' she said heavily. 'Oh, God, what a mess. I've sent the men home with nothing to do and I was going to have to lay them off at the end of the week because I couldn't give them any instructions—'

'I'm sorry.'

Her jaw dropped. 'I beg your pardon?'

'I said, I'm sorry—that it's been so difficult for you. I would have come sooner, but I've been in New York. I had them fax me the details of the deal when they came through, but to be honest I had no idea it was such a big site. We've acquired it as part of a company takeover, and I only saw the site plans this morning. Maybe I can give you some answers now, if you can spare me the time?'

She stared at him. She'd been that rude and he was apologising? 'Of course.' She nodded, but she didn't really have any time, because she had things to do—not least getting back to the bank with this latest bit of news—once she had worked out what the news was! She checked her watch. 'I can give you half an hour but I've got phone calls I have to make today, and footings that need to be marked out if I'm not going to get behind schedule,' she said, but he shook his head.

'No footings—and if you want this contract you can give me as long as I need, Ms Cauldwell. I don't want another brick laid or footing dug until I OK it. You can make your phone calls, but that's all. The rest of the day I want—and if I'm happy with what I hear, you get to keep the contract. If I'm not, you're out. Either way, there are going to be changes.'

She opened her mouth, shut it again and shook her head. Lord, it got worse, not better! 'I'll make sure you're happy, but I have to point out we're on a penalty clause—'

'Not if I stop you working. That would be

unfair. Anyway, I don't believe in penalty clauses, not if you trust your workforce. They shouldn't be necessary.'

Her jaw sagged again. 'Can I have that in writing?'

And to her utter amazement, he laughed. It changed his face completely, softening the harsh lines and crinkling the corners of his eyes and making them dance. And his mouth—that slow, lazy kick to one corner—

'By all means. Perhaps we could start again?' He stuck out his hand. 'Nick Barron. It's good to meet you, Ms Cauldwell.'

'Please, call me Georgie,' she said, putting her hand in his and wishing, just *wishing* she'd remembered to drown it in handcream that morning.

And then she forgot everything except the firm, hard grip of his hand, the warmth of his fingers and the sense of loss as he let it go.

'Right. I suppose you're going to want me to

put on one of those silly hats and wear a badge that says Visitor or something.'

'Something like that,' she said, her heart pitter-pattering at his smile and completely forgetting that only a few minutes ago she'd been ready to kick him off the site! Well, she'd got one more chance with him, one last chance to sort out this sorry mess and emerge from it with her father's dignity and business intact, and she had no intention of blowing it.

She straightened her shoulders, threw him a dazzling smile and gestured towards the site office. 'Right, let's go and get you kitted out and then we can start.'

It was amazing.

Nick stood on what in better days might have been a lawn, looking out over the sea and listening to the waves crashing onto the beach below. They were pounding the rocks of the sea defences, sending up great plumes of spray high over the prom, and the cold salt-laden wind was tugging at his hair and making him feel alive.

He laughed, just with the sheer exhilaration of the moment, and turned to Georgie, to find her watching him with a thoughtful expression on her face.

'What is it?'

'You love it too—the sea,' she said slowly, as if it really meant something to her, and he nodded.

'Especially at this time of year, when it's wild and windy and untamed.'

She turned and stared out over the pounding waves, and a little shiver ran over her. 'It scares me, but I can't live without it. It's dangerous and deceptive and wonderful and powerful and I wouldn't live anywhere else if you paid me.'

'So where do you live?'

She gave a rueful laugh. 'In my father's house in Yoxburgh at the moment, but it's only temporary. I'm going to buy one of these when they're finished. It's one of the reasons I agreed to help.'

Turning his back on the sea, he returned his attention to the site, studying it and trying to get a feel for it, and he began to think Tory might be right to be so excited.

A once-lovely Victorian house sat at the top of the slope, majestic in a rather shabby-chic kind of way, with bay windows and French doors facing the sea, and because of the curve of the bay they'd catch the sun all afternoon. He swivelled. The plot ended at a high retaining wall that held the garden back above the under-cliff road. The wall was about waist high on the inside of the garden, but well over head high on the other side, giving privacy without interfering with the view.

And the view from all the rooms must be spectacular, he realised, studying it again, but as if that wasn't enough, there was a square three-storey tower at the right-hand end, soaring up over the roof level of the main house, and the room at the top had windows on three sides.

It would make a fantastic look-out, a perfect place to sit and watch the ships going in and out of Felixstowe and Harwich further down the coast. There would be yachts, as well, and dinghies. He hadn't been here for years, but he'd been brought up only thirty or so miles away and he knew from day trips in his youth that it was a popular spot for sailors. He could picture the races that would take place in the summer, hear the children playing on the beach below, dogs chasing sticks into the sea—

And he was a romantic fool.

'Can we get into the house?'

'Sure. It's a mess—we've started stripping it out, so you have to look where you're going—'

'Don't worry, I won't sue you. I'm a firm believer in people making their own mistakes and taking responsibility for their own actions.

The litigation culture we're all getting into makes me livid. Whatever happened to common sense?'

Georgie snorted. 'Tell it to my father's insurers. They'd have hysterics if they could hear you talking.'

'No, they'd probably agree with me—or their underwriters would.'

She laughed. 'Maybe. Come on, we'll go in this way.'

They went in through an open door at the bottom of the tower, their footsteps echoing in the empty rooms, loud on the bare boards, and he tried to concentrate on the building, but the pint-sized fireball beside him was demanding his attention in ways he hadn't expected at all, and he was utterly distracted.

At first glance he'd mistaken her for a girl, but in here, without the sun in his eyes, he could see she was all woman. Not that the women he usually associated with would appreciate her

charms. Oh, no. There was no urbane sophis-
tication, no glitter and glamour and not a
designer label in sight, but this small, energetic
woman was so vitally alive she'd put all of
them in the shade.

'So what are the plans for this building?' he
asked, dragging his mind off the subtle curves
he could barely make out under her oh-so-sexy
luminous jacket.

'Two apartments in the original house, and a
small town house at this end with the tower, and
then the extension is destined to be four more
apartments. Come, I'll show you. The tower's
wonderful.'

It was. It was everything he'd imagined and,
as he'd thought, the view from the room at the
top was spectacular. It was nearly as spectacular from all the principle rooms at the front of
the house, as well, but as his guide took them
down a corridor and into the rear extension it
took a serious downturn.

This bit of the building was a much later addition, a dull rabbit-warren, the rooms small and uninteresting and not a patch on the front. He was much more interested in studying the way her hips swayed, the way she tossed her hair out of her eyes, and he could tell she wasn't interested in this part of the building either. This whole later addition to the house needed flattening, frankly, and he couldn't believe they weren't going to do that.

'Who's the architect?' he asked, cutting across a stream of facts that left him cold.

'Oh. Um—a man my father's never worked with before. He's a friend of Andrew Broomfield's, I believe.'

Nick nodded. That made sense. Another bad decision, taking on a friend to save money and ending up with a design without vision, cramming in as much profit-making potential as possible and losing the plot in the process.

'Can you go over the plans with me?'

'Of course. If you're very good, I might even conjure up a cup of tea.'

'Oh, I'm good,' he murmured without thinking, and she looked away, but not before he saw her eyes widen and soft colour touch her cheeks.

'I don't doubt it,' she said under her breath, and then, turning on her heel, she clomped out of the building in her ridiculous boots and vile yellow jacket, the little dog at her heels, and he followed her across the messy, stony site to the tin shed she called her office, feeling more alive than he had in years…

'You mentioned a phone call,' he said, and she wondered if she should tell him just how close the bank was to pulling the plug, or if she should spend a little more time getting him on-side and see if she could sweet-talk the bank for another day.

No. The time for that was over. 'The bank,' she said, and he nodded slowly and folded his

arms, propping his long, beautifully propor-
tioned body back against the wall and regard-
ing her thoughtfully.

'Are they pressing you very hard?'

She nodded. 'We've had to pay bills and
wages. Andrew said the money was coming—'

'But it hasn't, and you're in the doo-doo?'

She felt her lips twitch. 'You could say that.
They've given me until close of business today.'

'How much?'

'Pardon?'

'How much do you need now to get them
off your backs and enable you to clear
existing debts?'

She sat down at her desk a little abruptly. Was
he seriously going to write her out a cheque for
thousands of pounds just like that?

'A lot,' she said bluntly. She pulled the figures
towards her, did a few calculations and turned,
to find he was looking over her shoulder at the
calculator.

'Is that it?'

'Roughly. For now,' she said, and he nodded.

'I'll round it up a bit, give you some working capital and a bit of breathing room.'

She felt her jaw start to sag. 'But I thought you were going to decide if we were to complete the build—'

'I just did.' He punched buttons on his mobile, spoke briefly to someone called Tory and handed her the phone. 'My PA. Give her the details of your bank account,' he instructed. 'She'll get the money moved before close of business today.'

She could hardly speak for relief. Her father was lying in hospital waiting for open-heart surgery, worrying himself senseless, the workforce had been fantastic but they were running out of patience, the bank had done all and more that could be expected of them, and she hadn't drawn any salary for weeks.

With tears threatening, she gave Tory the

details she needed, handed back the phone and stared hard out of the window.

'Thank you,' she said, and sucked in a huge breath. It was meant to steady her, but it turned into a sob, and after a moment of stunned silence he propped his hips on the desk beside her, pulled her head against his chest and rubbed her back gently.

'Hey, it's OK,' he murmured.

She fought it for a moment, but the scent of his aftershave and the warmth of his body and the steady beat of his heart were too much for her, and she gave in and let him hold her as the tension of the last few weeks freed itself in a storm of tears the like of which she hadn't cried since her mother died.

Then, suddenly overcome by embarrassment, she pushed away, stood up and went outside, pausing on the steps and staring at the sea while she sucked in great lungfuls of the wild, salty air and felt it fill her soul.

It was going to be all right. It was. With Nick Barron on board, maybe the project would succeed after all and her father's whole career wouldn't go down the pan...

A tissue arrived in her hand, and she blew her nose vigorously and scrubbed her cheeks on the back of her hand. It was going to be all right. She wanted to scream it out loud, to run into the sea yelling it to the gulls screeching overhead—

'Would this be a good time for that tea?' he murmured.

'I've got a better idea,' she said, turning to him with a smile that wouldn't be held down any longer. 'There's a café round the corner—nothing fancy, no barista making designer bevvies, just good, strong filter coffee and the best BLT baguettes in the world. I reckon I owe you that at least—and I haven't had breakfast yet.'

'It's ten to twelve.'

'I know. My stomach's well aware.'

He grinned, dumped his hard hat on the desk and held out his hand towards the door.

'In that case, what are we waiting for?'

CHAPTER TWO

SHE WAS right. Good strong coffee, a glorious view—and Georgie.

She'd changed out of the dreadful rigger boots and put on a rather less blinding jacket, and suddenly she was just a pretty young woman with black smudges of exhaustion under her red-rimmed and fabulous green-gold eyes.

They'd ordered two of her BLT baguettes, and while they were cooking the waitress had brought them their coffee. He took his black, but Georgie had poured the whole pot of cream into hers, and now her hands were cradling her cup almost reverently and her nose was buried in it, savouring the aroma with almost tangible pleasure. He watched her inhale and sigh, a contented smile playing over her lips.

'Gorgeous,' she said, and he couldn't have agreed more.

'Talk to me about the plans,' he said, dragging his attention from the full, soft lips and hoping his confidence in her father's firm didn't prove misplaced.

Her nose wrinkled up. 'What about them?'

'What do you think of them?'

She met his eyes thoughtfully, then shrugged, the little snub nose wrinkling again. 'Too dense. Too pedestrian. The architect is dull as ditchwater.'

'So what would you have done?'

'Employed a better architect?'

'Such as?'

She shrugged and laughed. 'Me?'

That stopped him in his tracks. 'You're an architect?'

'Uh-huh—and before you ask, I am old enough.'

He felt a twinge of guilt, and winced apologetically. 'Sorry. I guess I had that coming to me. So tell me, why are you running your father's site?'

'Hobson's choice. He collapsed, and I was— what is it they say in the acting world?— resting. Between roles. Actually I was taking time out and thinking about my future, and thus available at zero notice. He needs a triple bypass, and he's in Ipswich Hospital waiting to be transferred to Papworth for the operation. I'm sure it was worry as much as anything that pushed him over the edge in the end. This project's been nothing but trouble since it started. Rubbish specification, no answers, nobody in control, nobody taking responsibility, but they put us on a hefty penalty clause because they thought it would speed things up.'

'Because they needed results fast to bail them out.'

She shrugged. 'It wouldn't have worked. The design's awful—the planners passed it, but I don't think they were happy. It's just a series of boxes. As it stands, even with the view, I don't think the individual units on the site will sell well at all. They don't deserve to.'

'So what would you do differently?' he asked, getting back to his original question. 'You must have given it some thought.'

She laughed again, the sound sending heat snaking through his veins. 'Endless, but none of it really formulated.'

'That's fine,' he said, forcing himself to concentrate. 'Just think out loud.'

'Now? Really?'

'Now. Really.'

She tipped her head on one side and grinned, and those gold flecks in her eyes sparkled with an enthusiasm that was infectious. 'Halve it,' she said. 'Far fewer houses, much better quality, and get rid of that hideous extension for starters. It needs a wrecking ball through it. Here—I can't describe it, I need to show you.' Grabbing a napkin, she rummaged in her pocket, and he held out a pen.

She flashed him a smile as infectious as her enthusiasm, and started to doodle and talk at the same time, and as she did so he found himself smiling. She was amazing. A tiny powerhouse, full of clever and interesting ideas, a lateral thinker.

And gorgeous. Utterly, utterly gorgeous.

Cradling his coffee in one hand, Nick hunched over her doodles and found himself totally distracted by the tantalising smell of shampoo drifting from her softy, glossy hair. Pretty hair. Nothing remarkable, just a light mid-brown but subtle rather than dull, threaded with fine highlights in palest gold and silver and swinging forwards as she bent her head, the blunt cut just above her shoulders giving it freedom.

Absently, she tucked it behind her ear and a

strand escaped, sliding free and hanging tantal-
isingly close to his hand. His fingers itched to
sift it, to see if it was really as soft and as sleek
as it seemed, and it took a real effort to lean
back, to shift away from her a little and force
himself to watch the swift, decisive movements
of the pen and see her vision take shape.

And then, once he'd managed to concentrate,
he was riveted.

'It's all going to be OK, Dad.'

Her father's brows furrowed. 'But I don't
understand—where did he come from?'

She laughed. 'I don't know—heaven, maybe?
I wasn't going to question him too deeply. He's
put money into the account, and I've checked
with the bank and it's certainly there. We're
even in the black.'

The furrows deepened. 'So what's the catch?'

'No catch. He's buying Andrew out, for
whatever reason, and we're now dealing with

him. And he hates the plans, and wants me to come up with some other ideas. He's put every-thing on hold—'

'But the penalty clause—'

'Gone. He's deleted it—doesn't believe in them. Dad, it's OK. Truly. Trust me.'

His eyes searched her face for any sign of a lie, but for once there wasn't one, not even a tiny white one, and with a great sigh he lay back against the pillows, closed his eyes and shook his head slowly, an unexpected tear oozing out from under one eyelid and sliding down his grizzled cheek. 'I really didn't think we'd get out of this one. I'm not sure I believe it.'

Georgie could understand that. She was still having trouble coming to terms with it herself.

'Believe it,' she told him firmly, and bent over to kiss the tear away, a lump in her throat. 'You just concentrate on getting better and leave it to me. I'll see you tomorrow.'

His eyes flickered open. 'You going already?'

'I've got work to do—plans to draw.'

He held her eyes for a while, then smiled and patted her hand. 'Good girl. You've been itching to get at it for weeks. Go and do your best.'

'I will. Don't worry, Dad. I'll do you proud.'

'You always do,' he said, his eyes sliding shut again, and with the lump in her throat growing ever bigger, she left him to his rest and went home. The light was blinking on the answering machine, and she pressed the button and a voice flooded the room. Her heart jiggled. Nick.

'Georgie, tried your mobile but it was off. You were probably at the hospital—hope everything's OK. Just wondering when we can meet up and go over your ideas. I'm going to be stuck in the office for the next few days, but if you can manage to get down to London in the next day or two we could get together here one evening. I've got a spare room, so if it's easier you can stay the night or I can book you into a hotel, whatever you prefer. Just give me an idea of when—the sooner the better really. I'd like to get this thing underway ASAP.'

Stay the night? *Stay the night?* Her heart jiggled again, and she pressed the flat of her hand over it and forced herself to breathe. In, out, in, out—

Stay the night?

In the spare room.

'Keep saying that,' she advised herself, and, putting the kettle on, she nudged the thermostat on the boiler, grabbed a packet of biscuits and settled down at her drawing board with a cup of tea and a head full of dreams...

'Nick?'

'Georgie—how are you?'

All the better for hearing his voice again after twenty-four long, hard hours, but he wasn't going to know that. 'Fine. Look, I've put some ideas together, but I don't think there's any point in going into too much detail until you see what I've come up with and I get a better feel for what you're expecting.'

'I agree. So are you able to get down here, because I'm really stuck at the moment?'

'Sure. When?'

'Any time. My evenings are all free. It's a bit late tonight; it's gone six already—how about tomorrow?'

Her heart thumped. 'Tomorrow?' she squealed. She'd been hoping for longer to tweak her ideas, but needs must and tomorrow was better than today! She got a grip on her voice. 'Um—I can do tomorrow, if you're not too busy—'

'What sort of time?'

'I need to see my father—I'll be able to get the train at about five-thirty, and it's just over an hour to Liverpool Street. Then however long to get to you from there. Seven-ish?'

'Great. I'll meet you at the tube.' He told her which station to head for. 'Ring me when you get there,' he told her. 'I'll come straight over. It'll take me five minutes from when I get your call.'

It took six, and every one of them was endless, but by then Georgie was in such a ferment a second seemed to take an hour and yet the day hadn't been long enough. She'd gone over the plans again and again, tweaking and fiddling, quickly dropped into the hospital to visit her father and then had to rush through the shower and leave her hair to drip-dry on the train.

So she had a slightly soggy collar on her coat, and as she hovered outside the tube station the March wind whipped up and chilled her to the marrow.

She was scouring the traffic and trying to guess the sort of vehicle he might be driving when a low, sleek sports car growled to a halt beside her and the door swung open. 'Jump in,' he said, leaning across with a grin and giving her a tantalising glimpse of his broad, hard chest down the open neck of his shirt, and she slid into the low-slung seat, hugely grateful that common sense had prevailed over vanity and she wasn't wearing a skirt.

'Nice car,' she said, trying not to think about the chest, and his grin widened.

'It's my one indulgence,' he told her, but somehow she didn't believe him. The man had the air of one who indulged himself just whenever the fancy took him, and she fancied it took him pretty darned often.

'Buckle up,' he instructed, and then shot out into the tiniest gap in the traffic with a squeal from the tyres and the sweetest, throatiest exhaust note she'd ever heard. Just the sound was enough to make her knees go weak. That and the fact that it could pull enough Gs to squish her into the leather!

'I'd love a car like this,' she said with a sigh, 'but it would get ruined on a building site and anyway, I'm not a millionaire playboy.'

'And you think I am?'

'Aren't you?'

'Fair cop. Guilty on at least one count,' he chuckled.

'There you are, then. Anyway, I'd look ridiculous driving it.'

'I think you'd look gorgeous driving it, but in this traffic it might not be a good idea to try for the first time.'

He shot down the outside of a queue, cut across the lights just as they were changing and whipped into the entrance of an underground car park before she could register their whereabouts. Moments later he was helping her from the seat and ushering her towards the lift, while she wondered if she'd ever master the art of extracting herself from his car without loss of dignity. Not that it would be a perennial problem, she had to accept. Sadly.

He was totally out of her league, light-years away from her in terms of lifestyle and aspirations, and so far the only things they had in common were a love of the sea, and his car.

Oh, and disliking the original plans for the site.

She began to feel more cheerful, and it lasted until he ushered her into the lift, inserted a keycard into a slot and whisked her straight past all the numbered floors. When the display read 'P', the door hissed open and she walked out of the lift and stopped dead.

'Oh, wow,' she said softly.

All she could see were lights—so many lights that the night was driven back, held at bay by the fantastic spectacle of tower blocks like giant glass bricks stood on end and lit from within, layer upon layer of them, explosions of stardust as far as the eye could see.

She could make out the wheel of the London Eye revolving slowly in the distance with Big Ben beyond, and—oh, more, so many more famous London landmarks stretched out in front of them—Norman Foster's gerkin, the old

Nat West tower, City Hall—with the broad black sweep of the Thames snaking slowly past, so close it must almost brush the foundations.

Wonderful. Magical. Stunning.

For a moment she thought they were on the roof, but then he touched a switch and she realised they were standing in a room, a massive open-plan living space with a sleek kitchen at one end and huge, squashy sofas at the other. Between them, the dining area over-looked the deck and the fantastic view beyond the glass walls. And they really were—acres of glass, almost featureless and all but invisible.

'Oh, wow,' she said again, and he smiled, a little crooked smile, almost awkward.

'I wondered if you'd like it.'

'I love it,' she said, running an appreciative hand over the back of a butter-soft brown leather sofa and wondering what on earth she was doing here in this amazing place. 'I'm surprised. I don't normally like this kind of thing, I've always thought they're a bit cold and unfriendly, but it just does it so well. And the view!'

'I bought it for the view. It's got a three-hundred and sixty degree deck. All the rooms open onto it.'

He touched the switch again and clever, strategic lighting lit up planters full of architectural foliage, artfully placed sculptures and even—

'Is that a hot tub?'

He pulled a face and nodded. 'Bit of an indulgence.'

'I thought the car was your only indulgence?' she teased, and he laughed.

'Oh, the tub isn't an indulgence, it's purely medicinal. I couldn't cope without it. After a stressful day at the office or a long flight, it's just fantastic. And anyway, not many people get to see my apartment so it's pretty much a secret vice, so it doesn't count,' he added with a grin.

She found that knowledge curiously comforting. Not that it was any of her business how many people he chose to entertain. Not at all. But somehow…

'Drink?'

'Tea would be nice.'

He nodded, put the kettle on and produced a couple of mugs. 'What about supper? Do you want to go out, or shall I order in? There's a restaurant downstairs that delivers.'

She didn't doubt it. So far she'd seen the car park and the view from his apartment, but that was enough. She had sufficient imagination to fill in the bits in between, and she just knew they'd be equally impressive.

'Here would be lovely,' she said, unable to drag her eyes from the view. 'And it'll give us more time to look at the plans,' she added, trying to stick to the plot.

'OK—have a look at the menu and choose something.'

She looked, blinked and handed it back. 'Anything. All of it. Just looking at it is enough to make me drool. I had a cup of tea for lunch and a biscuit for breakfast, and I'd settle for a bag of greasy chips right now.'

His mouth quirked. 'I think we can do rather better than that,' he said, and picked up the phone and ordered in a low, crisp voice, while she watched a little boat make its way slowly up the Thames and wondered what it would be like to live here all the time. He came over and stood beside her, two steaming mugs of tea in his hands, and held one out to her.

'Come outside and have a look,' he suggested, and the wall of glass slid effortlessly aside and he gestured for her to go out.

It was gorgeous. Huge, for the roof terrace of a London apartment block, and, as she walked all the way round past what must be the bedrooms and back to the doors they'd come out of, it gradually sank in just how much money he must have.

The car had been a bit of a giveaway, but his

one indulgence? She didn't think so. Not by a country mile.

And yet it was curiously homely. The furnishings were simple, the plants on the deck were well cared for, and she had the feeling he didn't take his privileged position for granted. Unless he just had a designer with a gift for homemaking and a gardener to keep the roof terrace in order. Goodness knows it was big enough to demand it.

And then there was that other indulgence that was purely medicinal, the cedar hot tub that kept drawing her eye. She could see it was made of solid wood, not one of the timber-clad moulded-acrylic ones which, although very comfortable and easy to install, just wouldn't have had the same understated dignity as the cedar planks.

This was like a huge, shallow barrel set into a raised area, and with the wooden lid in place it acted as a seat. She perched on it to sigh over the view again, and felt the warmth seeping through the timber. 'It's on!' she said, surprised, and he grinned.

'Of course. This is the best time of year for them. We can go in if you want—sit in it and unravel and talk about the plans.'

She did want to. She was aching to, but she didn't quite trust herself, and she wasn't sure of the clothing etiquette, and anyway, she was here to work, she reminded herself firmly.

'Don't you want to look at the ideas on paper first?' she said with a touch of desperation, and he shrugged and ushered her back inside, to her disappointment and relief. No, just relief...

'We'll look at them now while we eat. There's always later,' he added, and the relief gave way to a flutter of nervous anticipation.

'Maybe,' she agreed, and, picking up the long cylindrical case she carried her drawings in, she unscrewed the end and pulled the sketches out.

'They're only rough,' she warned, but he just

shrugged, helped her spread them out on the huge coffee-table and stood a little statue on one corner to hold it down.

She blinked. She recognised the artist, and that piece had probably cost more than she'd earned last year. Oh, dear God, why on earth had she let him talk her into this? There was no way he was interested in what she had to say. He was so far out of her league—

'Right. Talk me through them. What's this thing here?'

She dragged her eyes back to the plans, took a deep breath and launched her sales pitch.

'That was amazing!'

He laughed softly at her as she pushed her plate away and sighed with contentment. 'I said they did good food.'

'You lied. It was perfection. Good doesn't even begin to do it justice.'

'Coffee?'

She nodded. 'Please—if it's not too much trouble?'

'No trouble. Hot and strong, isn't it?'

His eyes smouldered for a second, and she felt her cheeks heat. He was only talking about the coffee, for heaven's sake! 'Please. With lots of cream, if you have it.'

'Sure.' He turned away, and she fanned her face and gulped in air. Actually…

'Would you mind if I had a walk round on the deck for a minute? I just love the view.'

'Of course not. Help yourself.'

She let herself out through the seamless glass and crossed over to the balcony rail, leaning on it and staring down in fascination at the lights on the river. She could hear the traffic far below, the sirens, the honking horns, a barking dog, but it all seemed somehow remote. She felt as if they were floating, removed in some way from the reality of it, and against the night sky the city below them sparkled like fairy lights.

It would be so wonderful to slip into the hot tub and just lie there, suspended above the city in a magic world—

'Your coffee's ready. Want it in or out?'

She turned towards him and laughed softly. 'Out, but it's chilly. We'd better have it inside.'

'We could go in the tub—talk through your ideas.'

In the subtle lighting she couldn't read his eyes, but the tension seemed to hang in the soft velvet air between them, as if the world was waiting for her answer.

'I haven't got a costume,' she said, groping for practicalities.

He shrugged. 'I won't look, and we don't have to have the underwater lights on. You could wear your underwear if you're feeling coy.'

'What about you?'

She saw the flash of his teeth in the darkness as he grinned. 'I'll preserve your modesty, Georgie. I'll even lend you a robe.'

She couldn't resist any longer. He took her back in, handed her a hugely fluffy towelling robe and a pile of towels, showed her into a bedroom the size of the average house and disappeared.

By the time she emerged from the French doors in her room and walked round the deck, the cover was off the tub, their coffees were perched on the side and he was nowhere to be seen. But the bubbles drew her, and, slipping off the robe, she dropped it on the deck and stepped down into the steaming water.

The heat made her catch her breath, then sigh with delight as she slid her shoulders under the surface and leant back against the side, her modesty preserved by the bubbling water. She could still see the city stretched out below through the misty air, watch the slow progress of a converted barge as it carried its boisterous cargo of partygoers on their evening out, but the steam and the bubbling of the water cut off all the sounds of the city and wrapped her in a magical cocoon.

No wonder he used the tub to unwind. If it was hers she'd never drag herself out of it!

'Warmer now?'

'Oh, you made me jump,' she said with a laugh, turning her head, and then wished she hadn't because he was just there, looming over her in the mist, dropping the robe that had been slung over his arm and lowering his long, beautifully honed body into the steaming, foaming water with a groan of ecstasy.

'Oh, bliss.'

Oh, indeed. And to think she'd imagined the view was perfect before!

He was taller than her, so the water didn't cover his shoulders, just left her a tantalising glimpse of his chest, the gleaming skin beaded with moisture and drawn tight over rippling muscle, the light scatter of hair over his pecs just enough to underline that abundant masculinity. He'd dropped his head back against the side, and the taut line of his throat and the jut of his jaw made her legs go weak.

In the spill of light from the living room she could see a pulse beating in the little hollow between his collar-bones, and she ached to lean over and touch her tongue to it, to lick away the tiny pool of moisture that had gathered there.

'Gorgeous,' she said, trying not to moan aloud. She tried to think of something to say, but it was difficult to think about anything other than his body, and she tucked her legs up tight under her because she was so afraid that they'd stray over there of their own accord and tangle with those long, muscular limbs...

'Coffee,' he said, opening his eyes and levering himself up, and, passing her her cup, he settled back against the smooth cedar planking and studied her over his mug. 'Tell me about yourself,' he commanded softly.

She laughed, a little surprised. 'There's nothing much to tell—'

'Nonsense. Start with the easy bit. Where were you born?'

Now, that was easy. 'Ipswich. My father was working in Yoxburgh when I was born, and I was brought up in a house with a sea view—if you climb up to the attic and crane your neck!'

He chuckled. 'Hence your love of the sea.'

'Not really. That came later, when I went on holiday to Cornwall and watched the waves smashing against the rocks. We don't have that up in Suffolk, unless they're imported rocks for the sea defences. It's all sand and alluvial deposits, but at least it means we get lovely sandy beaches, and I love walking on the prom at night and listening to the surf whispering in the sand. And of course on stormy days where there are sea defences you can shut your eyes and listen to the waves crashing on the rocks and you could be anywhere.'

'That's the beauty of the sea,' he murmured. 'It's truly global. The smell, the sound—it doesn't change, wherever you are in the world.' He paused, then went on, 'So tell me, why architecture?'

'Oh.' That was a change of tack. 'Um—well, my father was a builder, of course, so I suppose that influenced me. He'd missed a lot of school because of illness and so he didn't get to university. He'd always loved houses, though, and he loved being outside, so he went into building, and the sounds and smells of construction were in my blood from birth as much as the sea was. It wasn't a big step from building houses to designing them, conceptually, and I managed to get the grades to study architecture, so I started training.'

'And then found you didn't like it?'

'No, I love it,' she told him. 'Proper architecture. What I don't like, and what I was doing day in day out, was filling in the gaps in a town planner's scheme—x many two-bed units, y many three-bed and so on. Little boxes. It wasn't what I wanted, what I was interested in, but it paid the bills and I thought it would be OK for a while until the right job came up.'

'But it wasn't.'

She thought of Martin, and sighed. 'It might have been, for a while, but there were personal issues as well.'

'Your boss?'

How had he known? She nodded agreement. 'He had matrimonial problems. He brought them to me.' Two of them, aged six and three, dear little girls who needed their sick mother and latched onto Georgie like limpets. As did Martin—until his wife recovered from her illness and took them back. Then he'd dropped her like a hot potato.

'Sounds messy.'

'You'd better believe it.' And there was no way she was filling in the blanks for him. It was still too raw, too fresh to talk about, the shock in the girls' eyes as he'd told them she was leaving still too painful to remember.

'So you thought you'd take a career holiday and think about things?'

She laughed, on safer ground now. 'My father's been nagging me to go into business with him for ages. For the past ten years he's been building exclusive, one-off houses. He's got a great reputation—that's why Andrew wanted him to do the school development. He thought the Cauldwell name might give it a bit of an edge. But the development isn't up to Dad's usual standards—much too big, not nearly exclusive enough—'

'But that's changing. This design of yours has got far fewer units on it, and lots of open spaces, and you've got rid of that disgusting extension on the back of the house. That's the most significant thing.'

'We have to get it past the planners, and to do

that I have to draw up much more detailed plans—if you approve of it, that is.'

'I think so. There are one or two things I want to talk about, but in principle I like what you've come up with. I like it a lot. And I'll want to retain part of the house to keep as a weekend retreat for me and other people from the firm to use.'

Her heart fluttered. 'Which part?' she asked, knowing what he'd say before he spoke.

'The ground floor and the tower.'

Damn. She felt her face fall, but couldn't do anything about it. Maybe he wouldn't notice—

'What is it?'

Trust him. 'What's what?'

'You don't approve for some reason.'

She could feel her smile was wry, and gave up and confessed. 'I was going to buy the tower.'

'Ah.' His eyes were thoughtful, searching. 'How about the upstairs apartment instead?'

She smiled again, another twisted little parody. 'It's not the same.'

'No. I can understand that. In fact I've toyed with the idea of keeping the house intact, just one unit, but it's crazy. It would be wonderful, but it's so big, and I don't suppose that many families would want a house as big.'

'It wouldn't be cost-effective either, not compared to dividing it into three units,' she said, but there must have been something in her voice because he tipped his head on one side and studied her curiously.

'You agree with me, don't you?'

She smiled wistfully. 'Oh, yes,' she said softly. 'I think it would make a fantastic family house. I can hear it echoing with the laughter of children—I can see them running on the lawn, and hear them giggling, and in the evening I can imagine parties spilling out into the garden, the music and laughter and murmured conversations…'

'You're just an old romantic,' he teased laughingly, but there was a wistful look in his eyes and she wondered if his solitary and hectic life-style was what he really wanted, coming home alone at night to sit by himself in his hot tub and brood over what was missing in his life—

And now she really was crazy! How on earth did she know he was solitary? Or missing anything? He might entertain a different woman here every night of the week. Hectic, sure. But solitary? Not if the women of London had a say in it, she was certain!

'Are you married?' she asked suddenly, and he chuckled.

'Me? Hardly. I can't see a woman putting up with my lifestyle for many seconds.'

That hadn't stopped Martin's wife from marrying him, but it had probably been the thing that drove her over the brink and put her in a psychiatric clinic for months. That and his constant put-downs.

'Now what have I said?'

She pulled herself together and found a

smile. 'Nothing. I was thinking about someone else.'

'Your old boss,' he said with uncanny accuracy.

She didn't want to go there, so she just smiled
again and he shook his head.

'He must have been a real bastard.'

'He was.'

He stood up, the water streaming off his beautifully crafted body, and she felt her heart lurch
against her chest. 'Come on, time to get out or
you'll turn into a prune. We can have another
look at the plans before we go to bed, as well.
Are you happy in my guest room, or do you
want me to ring the hotel next door?'

Her heart hiccuped again. 'No, your guest
room's fine,' she said quickly. 'I'm sure the
hotel wouldn't be nearly as nice and the view
won't touch it. It's lovely here.'

His smile was crooked. 'I love it, too. Here—
your robe.'

And he held it out for her so there was

nothing she could do but stand up in front of him in her soggy, all-too-transparent under-wear and climb the steps, turning her back to him so he could slip the robe over her arms while her cheeks burned self-consciously.

But he didn't leave it there. He snuggled it round her neck, mopping her hair with the thick shawl collar, tucking it round her like a mother—or a lover.

And she was getting crazy, stupid ideas. She wrapped it firmly across her chest, tugged the belt tight and stepped down onto the deck, glancing up as she did so and catching a strange expression in his eyes.

No. She was dreaming. He wasn't remotely interested in her, and even if he was, she wouldn't be interested.

Would she? She turned away, and as she did her head started to swim. 'Oh—dizzy,' she said, just as he reached out and caught her.

'It's OK, it'll pass. You were in the tub for too

long—you aren't used to it. It can do odd things to your blood pressure. OK now?'

No. She wasn't OK. She was pressed up against the hard, muscled slab of his chest, her cheek against the damp, wiry curls that she hadn't been able to take her eyes off, and his arms were round her, cradling her firmly against him.

And the last thing she wanted to do was let go.

'I'm fine. Sorry,' she muttered, and pushed gently backwards out of his arms.

And it would have been fine if she hadn't lifted her head and met his eyes, but she did, and they were smouldering in the darkness of the night, and without a murmur she went back into his arms, sighing softly as his head came down and blocked out the stars.

His mouth was warm and firm and persuasive, his lips coaxing, and she opened to him, giving him access. He drew her closer, the velvet stroke of his tongue sending quivers of desire through her body and nearly taking out her legs.

She whimpered against his mouth and with a growl of need he deepened the kiss, his hands sliding round inside the front of her robe, letting in the cold night air so her skin tingled and her nipples peaked under the brush of his thumbs. Gasping with the sensation, dizzy with wanting, she arched against him, feeling the hot, hard strength of him, the very physical evidence of his response, and her fingers closed over his upper arms and clung.

'Nick,' she said raggedly, and then she felt something change, felt him pull back, ease away, lifting his head and resting his forehead against hers, his breathing fast and uneven.

'What the hell are we doing?' he muttered, and his hands fell away, drawing the edges of her gown together, turning her towards her room and giving her a gentle push. 'Go and get dressed, Georgie,' he said gruffly, 'before we do something we'll both regret.'

Oh, too late, Nick. Far, far too late.

Hugging the gown around her, she went.

CHAPTER THREE

SHE showered and dressed, taking her time even though spending any more time in hot water didn't seem exactly necessary. She felt she'd gotten herself into quite enough by throwing herself at him when he'd just been stopping her from falling over!

'Idiot,' she ranted for the hundredth time. 'Such an idiot! Why on earth would you think he'd be interested in you? He's only human, and you take almost all your clothes off and shove yourself in his face! Of course he kissed you, but he can have his pick, for God's sake, so why on earth would he bother with a little nobody like you?'

She yanked on her jeans, zipped them and

tugged her jumper down. She couldn't be bothered with shoes, although it was so long since she'd painted her toenails they'd forgotten what it was like to look pretty. And anyway, he'd seen her feet already. Seen a damn sight more than her feet, and walked away.

'Idiot!'

'Georgie? I've put the kettle on.'

'Coming,' she said, and, closing her eyes to steady herself, she sucked in her breath, opened the door and went out.

'Tea or coffee?'

No way. She wouldn't sleep tonight as it was, and she certainly didn't need any more caffeine! 'I don't suppose you've got anything herbal?'

'Camomile? My mother likes it so I keep some here for her. I can probably find it.'

'Please.'

He poured water into mugs, stirred and brought them over to where she was hovering by the dining table. He'd cleared it, and now he set the mugs down and stared at them.

For a while he didn't speak, but then he let his breath out on a sigh and said, very softly, 'I'm sorry I kissed you. I didn't plan this, you know.'

'I didn't think—'

'Of course you did. You're not stupid. It must have looked like the corniest seduction in the world.'

'Hardly. Anyway, I can't really blame you when I was parading around in front of you in my underwear, for heaven's sake, but I certainly didn't think you'd planned it. I can't imagine you'd be interested enough to plan it—'

'What?' He raised his head and stared down at her with a bemused expression on his face. 'You didn't think I'd be *interested?* Are you crazy?'

She shrugged, embarrassed now. It had been bad enough outside in the dark, but now, with the light on—she looked away. 'Why would you?'

He cupped her chin in his fingers and turned

her back to face him, his eyes tender. 'Because you're funny and complicated and beautiful and intriguing—'

'Really?'

'Really,' he said emphatically, and then repeated it softly for good measure. '*Really.*'

She couldn't stop the smile. It started somewhere near her toes and spread all over her body, lighting up every sad and lonely part of her that Martin had left shrivelled and afraid, and she laughed and reached up, lifting her head to meet his halfway as she feathered a kiss of thanks onto those gorgeous, mobile, clever lips of his.

'You're pretty hot yourself.'

And he laughed and hugged her, then let her go and pushed her into a chair and pulled out her plans.

'Come on. Back to work. I've got an early start tomorrow and I want you to have enough information to be going on with for a while. I'll come up again at the weekend and maybe we can spend a bit longer together just having fun.'

And why not? She'd been hibernating for months, hiding from life, and for the first time in ages she *was* having fun. Safe, uncomplicated fun.

Safe? Uncomplicated?

Was she mad?

The train journey back to Suffolk later that morning gave her more than enough time for reflection, and with Nick's delectable body out of reach there was nothing to distract her from the cold, hard facts.

One: he was incredibly, unbelievably rich and powerful. And he held their future, hers and her father's, in his hands. She must be nuts to mess with him. If she'd tried she couldn't have found anyone more dangerous and complicated to get involved with.

Two: he could have anyone he wanted. He

probably did, on a regular basis. So he thought she was funny and complicated and beautiful and—what was the other one? Intriguing. Huh. At the moment. But it wouldn't last. Why should it? He'd soon get bored, cease to be intrigued, and then her heart would be in shreds all over again.

Oh, God. Even the thought made her shudder.

Thank goodness he'd stopped in time, because as sure as eggs she wouldn't have done. What on earth had she been thinking about? She'd *never* done anything like that. Never slept with a man she didn't know incredibly well, and she'd been right on the verge of doing such a thing for the first time in her life. If it hadn't been for his gentle but firm rejection, she might even have begged him.

Stupid, stupid girl. And so sudden! It had been months before she'd succumbed to Martin, not mere hours.

Not that she'd known Martin well, for all that.

Hardly. She'd thought she did, but it turned out she hadn't known him at all, and look where that relationship had got her.

You'd really think she'd have learned her lesson, but oh, no. In again, head first, without thought—

'You need locking up.'

The man sitting opposite her gave her a startled look and went back to his paper, and she coloured furiously and dug a notebook out of her bag.

She spent the rest of the journey writing down over and over again all the reasons why it would have been such a lousy idea to have slept with him, and bitterly regretting that he hadn't given her the chance.

And when she arrived home there was a delivery van outside, and a cheerful woman climbed out.

'Are you Ms Cauldwell?'

She nodded.

The woman disappeared into the back of the van, and emerged with a large box. 'For you.'

She took the box, signed for it and went inside, puzzled.

'Flowers', it said on the box. 'This Way Up'.

Oh, lord. She opened the box with trembling fingers to reveal a cloud of gypsophila and eucalyptus leaves. That was all. Nothing else, no roses or chrysanths or anything like that. Just gypsophila and leaves. She removed the arrangement in its beautiful, simple crystal vase and stared at it.

It had to be from Nick. Who else? There was a little card tucked into the arrangement, and she slipped it out of the envelope and read it.

'You take my breath away.'

Of course. The other name for gypsophila was baby's breath. Her eyes filled with tears, and she started to laugh.

'Oh, Nick,' she said. 'Just when I'd talked some sense into myself.'

She sent him a text.

Thanks. They're gorgeous.

His reply was almost immediate.

Glad you like them. What are you doing later? Got through work quicker and have more ideas.

Visiting her father, having another look at the plans, trying to get something more formal to go to the planners with…

Nothing.

Your place or mine?

She looked around her. Her father's house was lovely, in a quiet, leafy road in the old part of Yoxburgh, but in comparison to his apartment it was dated and shabby and needed a serious injection of time and money. Since her mother had died he'd lost interest, and the house reflected that.

But maybe Nick needed to see where she came from, needed reminding of how far out of her league he was, before she got in too deep.

Don't be stupid, she told herself fiercely. Nick didn't need any reminders, she did, but at least the house was clean now and she didn't want to leave the dog with the neighbour again, because it wasn't fair on either of them.

Mine. Ring me when you reach Ipswich.

And in the meantime, she had things to do— not least a visit to the supermarket as soon as she'd collected Archie from the neighbour. She'd eaten everything remotely edible in the house while she'd been working on the plans, and now there wasn't even a teabag left.

And there were no sheets on the spare bed.

She rummaged in the airing cupboard, came up with nothing respectable and went shopping. Two hours later, with the fridge groaning, the new bedding in place after the quickest of quick washes and a blast in the drier, and with Archie banned from the bedrooms, she went to the hospital to visit her father, to be greeted with the news that he was about to be transferred to Papworth and was having his operation in the morning.

'That's wonderful!' she told him, wishing now that Nick wasn't coming tonight and she could give her father her full attention.

'Is that your phone?'

'Oh, rats, I forgot to turn it off. I'll be back in a minute.' She scrambled for the phone and hurried out of the ward, answering the call with trembling fingers. 'Nick—hi,' she said breathlessly. 'I was going to ring you—'

'You said to call from Ipswich.'

Her heart skittered. 'You're here already?'

'Here? Where are you, then?'

'I'm at the hospital with my father. He's about to be transferred to Papworth—they're doing his operation tomorrow.'

'Were you expecting that?'

'No—not just yet. I mean, I hadn't really thought—'

'I'd like to meet him—can I do that?'

Her heart bumped against her ribs again. 'He's not really up to talking much about the development—'

'Georgie, credit me with a little sense,' he said softly. 'I was hoping to reassure him— take some of the worries away, if I can.'

And it was a wonderful idea, of course. 'Well— if you don't mind, that would be very kind.'

'I can be,' he said wryly. 'When I'm not plotting the seduction of innocent virgins.'

Her cheeks coloured and she laughed softly. 'I'm sorry.'

'No, I'm sorry. What ward is he on? I'll come and find you.'

She gave him directions and met him in the corridor ten minutes later, wondering how to greet him, but he didn't give her time to think, just pulled her into his arms and hugged her, getting to the heart of it without hesitation.

'Are you OK?'

'Why wouldn't I be?'

'Because your father's about to have open-heart surgery?'

She felt the apprehension return and bit her lip. 'I'm OK now.'

His grip tightened for a moment, and she felt his lips brush her hair before he released her and turned towards the ward door. 'Is this it?'

'Yes. Come on in, I'll introduce you to him. I think he's quite anxious to meet you.'

'How is he about the operation?'

'Scared.'

He pulled her to a halt, kissed her softly and

straightened her hair, tucking a loose strand behind her ear with gentle fingers. 'He'll be all right. Deep breath,' he said, and she took his advice, calmed herself and flashed him a smile.

'Thanks. Come on.'

She led him to her father's bedside.

'Dad, this is Nick Barron. Nick, my father, George.'

Nick held out his hand. 'It's good to meet you, sir. I've heard a lot about you.'

Her father looked at his new visitor searchingly, and then took his hand in a grip that Georgie knew wouldn't be nearly as firm as he would have liked.

'Good to meet you, too. Put a face to a name. Georgie's been telling me about you, but I'm glad of a chance to get to meet you—make sure the business is as safe as she says it is.'

'It's safe, I promise you,' he said sincerely, and Georgie felt her eyes fill as he quietly and confidently put her father at his ease. 'I've heard some very good things about your work, and I'm looking forward to working with you on the development when you're feeling fitter. In the meantime, Georgie seems to have things very much under control. She's a very capable young woman.'

'She's a good girl.' George Cauldwell studied Nick frankly, then nodded. 'She said you were all right. Said we could trust you.'

'You can.'

'She said you didn't like the plans.'

'I don't—but I like her ideas. I like them a lot. She's got real vision. It'll be much better.'

'You'll have to convince the planners,' he said doubtfully, but Nick just chuckled and threw Georgie a smile that could have melted her socks.

'Oh, I think Georgie can do that. Frankly they don't stand a chance. They'll be sitting ducks— they won't know what's hit them.'

'That's my girl.' George chuckled and patted

his daughter's hand. 'I see you've got her worked out.'

'Oh, I never underestimate a woman. I've been well trained by my PA,' he said with a wry smile, and her father laughed and relaxed back against the pillows, looking better than he'd looked in months.

Nick reached into his pocket. 'I brought you this—I don't know if you're into it, but I thought it might help to pass the time.' He pulled a little book out and handed it to George.

'Sudoku! I'd never heard of it, but I've been sitting here bored to death and I've taken to doing the puzzle in the paper. And this is a whole book? That should stop my mind addling completely. Thank you. That's very good of you.'

'My pleasure.' He stood up. 'Right, I'm going to get out of your hair and leave you with your daughter.'

She felt a stab of disappointment. 'Oh— where are you going?'

'Nowhere. I thought I might find a coffee while you pack your father's things, and then if you want to go with him to Cambridge I thought I could drive you.'

She felt tears prick her eyes. 'You don't have to do that.'

'I know—and if you don't want me to, I won't, but if it helps…?' His shoulders lifted in a little shrug, and she bit her lip and nodded.

'Thank you. That would be really helpful. But you don't have to leave us.'

His smile was gentle. 'Yes, I do. You go and sort him out and I'll come back in half an hour. Ring me if you need me sooner.'

And he was gone, striding down the ward while she stared helplessly after him, fighting back the tears.

'He's a good man,' George said gruffly. 'Thoughtful. Decent.'

She nodded. 'He is,' she said, her voice uneven. A lot more decent than she had any right to expect, but she wasn't getting into that with her father! She dusted off her hands. 'Right, come on, let's tackle this locker of yours.'

'Thank you so much for driving me.'

'You're welcome. Georgie, he'll be all right. They'll take good care of him there.'

'I know. I'm just scared.'

She opened the car door and unravelled herself from the depths of the seat, wondering if she'd ever work out how to do it gracefully. Like everything else, Nick made it look so effortless.

'Nice house.'

She closed the car door and looked up at her family home fondly. 'I think so, but I'm biased. I grew up here.'

'I thought you had a sea view?'

She laughed. 'We do, from the attic. Anyway, as I said, it's not much more than a glimpse and you get a crick in your neck to see it.'

He laughed with her and took a soft leather

bag from the boot, then followed her inside. 'Where shall I put this?'

'Just dump it there. We can take it up later.'

Their eyes met, and despite all her worries about her father, despite the fact that she was tired and wanted a shower and something to eat, somehow his arms seemed the best place in the world to be at that moment, and he was holding them open to her.

'Come and have a hug,' he murmured, reaching for her, and she settled against his chest and wondered what on earth she'd done to deserve him.

His voice was a soft rumble under her ear. 'I missed you today.'

'I missed you, too,' she confessed, even though she'd had no intention of telling him any such thing, but after all he'd gone first, and anyway it was only the truth.

'Why don't you go and run yourself a bath while I cook us something?' he said, holding

her at arm's length and looking down into her
eyes with gentle understanding.

'You don't know what there is, and Archie's
in the kitchen—he'll lick you to death.'

'I'm sure I can cope with him, and as for the
food, I'll work it out. At least if you've bought
it I know you'll eat it.'

So she went into the bathroom, contemplated
the luxury of the bath and opted instead for the
speed of the shower, so she could get back
downstairs to him, because she didn't want to
waste a single minute.

Scrubbed and shiny and with her hair more
tumble- than blow-dried, she doused herself in
body lotion, drowned her hands in intensive
repair treatment guaranteed to bring her skin back
from the brink of disaster, and spritzed herself
with the last dregs of her favourite perfume.

Now what? Clothes? Nightclothes? She
thought with affection of her jersey pyjamas,
and laughed softly to herself. Hardly sexy, but

her wardrobe was deeply lacking in sexy little numbers for seducing multimillionaire play-boys, and anyway, as he'd pointed out last night, it wasn't what he wanted, so she settled for a pair of comfy old jeans and a snuggly sweater, and ran downstairs, to find him chopping vegetables with the phone tucked under his ear.

'Tory, you're a big girl, just deal with it,' he was saying, and she wondered what Tory was being expected to deal with. Ordering more pens, or the takeover of another company? It could have been either, she thought, and realised she knew very little about him other than that he seemed genuinely kind.

However, you didn't get to be a millionaire without treading on a few underdogs, she told herself, just as he turned and shot her a grin. 'Sorry, Tory, got to go. I've got a hot date with a salmon steak and it won't wait. I'll talk to you again tomorrow.'

He switched off his phone, slid it back into his pocket and took a bottle of wine out of the fridge. 'I've just arranged to have the day off tomorrow so I can go to Cambridge with you. Tory was having a bit of a hissy fit, but she'll get over it. Chablis?'

'That wasn't in there,' she said, staring at the wine and remembering that she'd failed to buy any, and then added, 'You didn't have to do that—take the day off for me.'

'Yes I did. And no, the wine wasn't in there. It was in my car.'

'Oh. It won't be cold enough—'

'It's fine. I've got a refrigerated glovebox.'

Of course. To chill champagne. Silly her.

'Then thank you, wine would be lovely—and thank you for taking the day off. I hope Tory will forgive me.'

'She'll be fine. Georgie, what's the matter? Is it tomorrow?'

She laughed and closed her eyes, shaking her head. 'I just have no idea how you live—what you do, what makes you tick. How your day works.'

'Like yours, I imagine. I go to bed, I get up, I go to work, I get home, I cook a meal or if I can't avoid it I go out for dinner, and I go to bed. If I'm really lucky, it's my own and not in the company apartment in New York or a hotel in Osaka or Shanghai or Timbuktu.'

His voice was light, but there was an underlying thread of something she recognised. She put her hand on his arm, rubbed it lightly without thinking. 'You make it sound awful.'

'It is awful. I hate it. I'm sick of it.'

'So why do it?'

He laughed softly. 'Because I don't have any choice. Because I have a business to run, and people depending on me, and I can't just cop out and skive off.'

'You did this afternoon—and you're doing it tomorrow.'

His eyes softened. 'Yes. I did today—and I will tomorrow. For you. Come here.'

He folded her into his arms and hugged her. 'You smell gorgeous—shampoo and perfume and Georgie. Fabulous.' He kissed her lingeringly on the lips, then eased away with a sigh and handed her a glass of wine. 'Here, wrap yourself round that while I finish off the supper. I take it nothing in the fridge was reserved for anything special?'

She shook her head. 'Only for you coming.'

His smile melted her heart. 'Thank you.' He gave her a little push. 'Go and sit down at the table and stop distracting me.'

So she sat at the table with her flowers in pride of place in the centre and Archie leaning against her leg and gazing adoringly at Nick, and together they watched him chop and slice and sliver, using the cheese slicer to make ribbons of courgette and carrot which he steamed in a sieve over a pan of water with a few mangetout peas while he flashed the salmon steaks in butter and lime juice and checked the baby new potatoes with a fork.

The smells were mouth-watering, and by the time he'd served it up and set it down in front of her she was ready to marry him.

And that was a shocking thought. So shocking that for a moment she couldn't move. Couldn't eat, couldn't breathe, couldn't even look at him, because it had just hit her with all the subtlety of an express train.

He picked up his wine glass and held it out to her. 'To us,' he said softly, and she picked up her glass and touched it to his, and echoed,

'To us,' but her smile was automatic and the wine could have been water.

She was in love with Nick Barron, and nothing in her life was ever going to feel the same again…

CHAPTER FOUR

HER father's operation went without a hitch, and after it was over and he was back on the ward, Nick took her home and fed her and hugged her while she cried, then they went down to the site with Archie and talked about it some more, then went for a walk along the prom and had coffee in her favourite café while Archie sat patiently outside and waited for them to stop being boring and take him for another walk.

Which they did, because the tide was out by then and they could get almost all the way round the point, scrambling over the rocks that were piled against the old sea wall to stop the constant erosion.

'Can you ever get all the way round?' he asked, and she nodded.

'Sometimes, if it's a very low tide and you catch it right, but not usually. And it's slippery and dangerous—not that that ever stopped me. I used to climb the sea wall when I was a kid and work my way round over the waves, but the rocks weren't here then and it was safer if you fell. You just got wet.'

He looked at the ten-foot-high sea wall and whistled softly. 'It hasn't got any hand- or foot-holds.'

'Oh, it has,' she said. 'If you do it in bare feet it's OK.' And the daredevil in her kicked off her shoes, tugged off her socks and scaled the wall with ease, leaving him open-mouthed and laughing at the bottom. She turned and grinned down at him, victorious, and chanted, 'I'm the king of the castle,' and he stood there with his hands on his hips, shaking his head at her and smiling while Archie leapt at the wall and whined, desperate to join her. Which was more than could be said for Nick.

He shaded his eyes and looked up at her. 'You're mad, woman. For God's sake, come down before you fall.'

'I won't fall,' she said confidently. 'It's not that high, Nick.'

'No—it's just featureless! How the hell can you stay up there?'

She laughed. 'Oh, this is easy. Hanging my bra from the lightning conductor on the dome on top of the tower at my school was much more of a challenge.'

He shuddered. 'You must be a spider. I knew there was something strange about you.'

'Sticky pads on the hands and feet,' she said with a grin, slithering back down and landing lightly on the rock beside him. 'Just do me a favour and don't ever tell my father what I used to get up to—he'd have a fit.'

'I'm sure,' Nick said drily. 'I should imagine you were a real handful to bring up.'

'Not really,' she said, dusting off her feet and tugging her socks and shoes back on. 'I just made sure they had no idea what I was up to. Much easier.'

'Hmm. I didn't employ that principle until I was much older.'

'And I bet you were much worse.'

'But different.'

'What? Fast cars? Women? Drugs?'

'Never drugs.'

But he didn't deny the others, and she could imagine him as a young man, a daredevil with the girls flocking round him, begging him to take his pick. She was absurdly jealous of them all.

They turned back, strolling side by side, Nick holding out his hand for her and steadying her on the slippery rocks, then not letting go after they reached the safety of the sand again. They went down to the water's edge, on the firm, hard sand, and skimmed pebbles on the flat surface of the sea. And he beat her.

'Well, I've got to be good at something,' he said with a smile, and she thought of the searing kiss he'd given her by the hot tub on Wednesday night, and just knew that skimming pebbles wasn't the only thing.

'My mother used to be good at this,' she said, hefting a little flat pebble in her hand and refusing to let herself think about his kisses. 'She used to win all the time.'

She brushed the sand off her hands, the memory touching her with sadness, and he threaded his fingers through hers and started strolling back up the beach again.

'You've never mentioned her before,' he said quietly. 'What happened to her?'

'She died five years ago.' Funny how it still hurt so much, even after all this time. 'She had cancer. We only knew for a few weeks before she died, but it was horrible to watch.'

His fingers tightened slightly, squeezing hers. 'I'm sorry. I know how that feels. My father died of MS when I was ten. That was pretty dreadful, but I grew up with it and I suppose it happened so gradually I just got used to it. My friends found it harder to deal with than I did. I just took the bedpans and so forth for granted. They were part of life, but it was awful to watch him suffer, and it was a relief when he died. Then we only had the guilt to deal with.'

His smile was wry and twisted, and she pulled him to a halt and hugged him. 'I'm sorry,' she murmured, and he sighed and hugged her back.

'Me, too. Life's a bitch, et cetera.' He let her go, sliding his hand down her arm and threading his fingers through hers again. 'So—any brothers or sisters?'

'One brother, David, in Australia. He's into surfing, and decided he might as well go where it was good. Dad hoped he'd go into the business, but he was never interested. What about you?'

'One sister—bit of a loose cannon. She's got two boys from different relationships, neither of them in touch with their fathers, and the last I heard she'd broken up with her wealthy Brazilian boyfriend, is pregnant again and coming to live with my mother not far from here—just the other side of Framlingham, but how they'll all fit in my mother's tiny cottage I have no idea. She's an artist, and the idea of Lucie's two little tearaways rampaging through her studio makes me wince.'

Georgie laughed. 'Sounds horrific. Poor woman.'

'Oh, she loves them all to bits, but it'll drive her mad after a while. It always does. It won't last. I give it three weeks before I have to go in there and mediate!'

Laughing, they made their way back to her car, Archie sopping wet and covered in sand, and Nick looked at him and raised a brow.

'Glad it's your car,' he said, and she chuckled.

'I had good reasons for bringing it,' she told him, and, clipping Archie back into his harness on the back seat, she drove back to the house.

'I ought to go back and see Dad,' she said, worrying her lip, and he glanced at his watch.

'It's nearly five. I need to give Tory a ring, and then do you want me to drive you?'

She did, but she didn't want to seem needy and pathetic. It was just that the sight of her father lying there smothered in tubes and wires—

'Georgie, it's no big deal. If I don't drive you I'll come with you, unless you'd rather I didn't, in which case I'll follow you, but I'm not leaving you. Not now. Not unless you ask me to.'

She shook her head. 'Sorry, not a chance. I'd love you to drive me. And when we get back we ought to have another look at the plans.'

But they didn't. It was past ten by the time they arrived home, and while he made a couple of phone calls she took Archie for a quick walk round the block. When she went back in, he handed her a glass of wine, hung up the dog's lead and took her into the sitting room. He'd lit the fire—only a gas one, a coal-effect thing that had real flickering flames, but it made the room cheery on a chilly night, and it was yet another thoughtful touch.

He sat down at one end of the sofa and patted the cushion beside him. 'Come here,' he commanded softly, and she snuggled up against him, sipping her wine and staring into the flickering flames, emotionally drained.

'He looked awful, didn't he?'

'He'll be fine, Georgie. They said he's doing really well. The first few days were bound to be rough.'

'He's just always been so strong, so fit. It's such a shock to see him like that.'

'He'll soon be stronger. You wait and see.'

'Mmm.' She sipped her wine, snuggled closer and wondered what this week would have been like without him. It was Friday. She'd met him on Monday, when he'd wiped out their debt at a stroke, seen him again with the rough plans on Wednesday, almost fallen into bed with him, and now forty-eight hours later she was curled up with him in front of the fire, her father's operation had apparently been a success, and she couldn't imagine life without Nick.

Just like that, her life had been transformed, with him at the heart of it. Without him the bank would have foreclosed, her father would have been recovering from his operation with bankruptcy proceedings in the offing, and what that would have done to him she couldn't even begin to think.

She turned her head and looked up at him, and he glanced down and smiled.

'Thank you,' she said, her voice so choked she could hardly speak. 'Thank you for everything you've done.'

'Oh, Georgie,' he said softly, and, taking her

wine and setting it down on the table, he shifted so he was lying beside her, his arms around her holding her close, and his lips brushed hers tenderly.

'I don't know what we would have done—'

'Shh. You would have been all right.'

'No. No, Nick, we wouldn't. Without you—'

'But you aren't without me, so don't think about it.'

'I can't help it—'

'Then I'm not doing my job properly,' he murmured, and his lips found hers, sealing in her protest and driving everything except him right out of her mind…

The next few weeks flew by.

The plans were passed by a relieved planning committee who were glad to see the changes and admitted to having had reservations with the previous scheme, and the hideous extension on the back of the house had gone.

So had her hopes of having the tower house, but her father was home, growing stronger by the day, and he was delighted with the new scheme too, so things were looking up hugely.

And every time she wanted an answer to a query, she phoned Nick or asked him when she saw him, which was most weekends.

At first he'd come up to her, staying in the spare room and entertaining her father, looking over the site, ironing out minor queries. Then, as her father grew stronger, she was able to go down to London for the weekend. Just for Saturday night because she didn't like to leave her father for longer, but they were growing closer by the day, and she'd stopped wondering what Nick saw in her and started to believe that he really did care.

She wondered what they'd do. Would he take her out for dinner? Would they eat in his apartment?

Would they become lovers?

Yes. If he suggested it, she knew they would. She'd thought, after Martin, that she'd never have another relationship as long as she lived, but Nick was so different, so open and honest and funny, utterly straightforward. She trusted him. That was the difference—and it made all the difference.

'I hope you've got party clothes in that bag,' he said when he picked her up. 'We're going out tonight to a friend's party—I'd forgotten about it, but it's been booked for ages and it's only round the corner. We just need to stick our heads in.'

Oh. So, not a nice, quiet night in, dallying in the hot tub, then. She felt a twinge of disappointment, but in fact it was fun, and they did a lot more than stick their heads in.

The party was in a neighbouring apartment block and it was in full swing by the time they arrived at ten, after a leisurely dinner. He ushered her in, arm around her shoulders in a proprietorial gesture she found curiously touching, and, steering her through the crowd with a few words of greeting here and there, he took her over to meet Tory, his PA.

'Tory, look after Georgie while I get her a drink, and don't tell her anything too dreadful about me,' he threatened, and left them alone together.

'So you're Georgie,' Tory said with a grin, and hugged her. 'I have to thank you—you've turned Nick into a reasonable human being again. He'd been getting really grouchy, and just recently I've even caught him whistling. So good on you. Well done. And I love the new plans, by the way. Soooooo much better! And talking of better, how's your father?'

She laughed, caught up in Tory's infectious, bubbly mood and blown away by her welcome. 'Much better, thanks. Improving every day. I'm sorry I stole Nick from you at such short notice when he was having his op.'

Tory flapped her hand dismissively. 'I can cope, he knows that. I just whinge a bit if he does it too often, but to be honest he's so much easier to deal with now it's a small price to pay. I hope you're going to stick around.'

Georgie was amazed. She didn't know what she'd expected of Tory, but this pretty, dynamic young woman with crazy hair and sparkling eyes wasn't it. For a moment she wondered if she should be jealous, but then Tory introduced her to their host, a guy called Simon Darcy, and one look at the sizzle between them put all such thoughts out of her mind. And anyway, Tory sounded as if she wanted Georgie to stay in Nick's life—something she was more than happy to do!

'You OK?'

She turned and smiled up at him. 'Fine. I've just been getting the low-down on you from Tory.'

'I don't doubt it,' he said drily, and shook Simon's hand. 'Hi there. Good party.'

'Glad you could make it. And it's good to meet the woman who's tamed you. It's about time,' Simon said with a chuckle, and Georgie blinked.

Tamed him? Her?

Nick's arm closed around her shoulders and he grinned. 'You can talk. Let's get one thing clear. I don't care what you and Tory get up to out of office hours, she's my PA and you can't have her!'

'I might make her an offer she can't refuse,' Simon said, and Tory laughed and sparkled up at him, and Nick groaned.

'Oh, no. Tory, don't fall for it, he's just pretending to like you so he can steal you from me. It's all lies.'

'But such pretty lies,' she said, still sparkling. 'And at least he appreciates me.'

'I appreciate you!'

Tory snuggled closer, her eyes bright with mischief. 'Not like Simon.'

Nick shook his head and turned to Georgie. 'It's sickening. Come on, let's go and dance.'

And that was it. She spent the rest of the evening in his arms, and if they weren't dancing he had his arm firmly round her shoulders, hugging her against his side while they chatted to his friends. She could have stayed there forever like that, but just after midnight the music dropped down a gear, the lively dance music giving way to smoochy, sexy love songs, and with a sigh he drew her even closer, bending his head so they were cheek to cheek. His lips brushed her hair, sending shivers through her, and they were so close she could feel the steady, solid pounding of his heart under her ear.

They hardly moved. Their weight shifted from foot to foot, their bodies so close they could have been one.

Should have been one.

And when Nick lifted his head and stared down into her eyes, the heat in them sent flames ripping through her body, depriving her of oxygen so she couldn't speak. All she could do was nod, the tiniest movement of her head, but it was enough.

They left without a word to anyone, her hand held firmly in his as he all but dragged her into the empty lift and hit the button for the ground floor before turning her into his arms and holding her hard against his chest in a tense and charged silence.

He didn't kiss her, didn't really touch her except to hold her, but she could feel the tension in him, feel the pounding of his heart and the unmistakable pressure of his arousal, and her knees started to tremble. She needed him so much, had been waiting for this moment for weeks, but now it was here she started to fret.

What if she disappointed him? What if it was only the anticipation that was keeping him interested? The lift doors slid open, and he marched her along the pavement, into the lift at his apartment block and then back into his arms.

His chest was heaving, and she didn't think her legs would hold her up for many more seconds, but then the lift door opened and they were in his apartment, the harsh white light of the full moon slashing through the darkness and touching everything with an eerie silver.

And then, quite unexpectedly, he let her go and went over to the doors, opening them and going out onto the deck, his hands gripping the rail as he stared down into the oily black water of the Thames.

She followed him, laying a trembling hand against his shoulder. His knuckles were white, and she could feel the tension coming off him in waves. 'Nick?'

'Are you sure about this?' he said, turning abruptly to her and spearing her with his dark, wild eyes. 'Because I can stop now, but once I touch you again—'

'I'm sure.'

For a moment he didn't move, but then the air

left him in a rush and he reached for her, easing her into his arms with surprising restraint. 'Thank God,' he whispered, and his mouth found hers and she lost all rational thought. Lost everything except the need to be close to him, to touch him, to feel him…

'Are you OK?'

She turned her head towards him and smiled with the last flicker of her energy.

'Wonderful,' she murmured. 'You?'

'Amazing.' He shifted, reaching for her and easing her closer. 'You're amazing.'

No. She wasn't amazing. She was amazed. Amazed by his strength, his stamina, the sheer masculine power of his body, the tenderness of his touch, the warmth of his caresses. She'd never felt so special, so important, so cared for.

So cherished.

She wriggled even closer, so that their bodies

touched from head to toe, and with a contented sigh she fell asleep.

She was woken later by a phone ringing, and opened her eyes. Nick was sitting on the edge of the bed, his back to her, and she rolled towards him and listened, wondering who was calling him at this time of the night.

'I'll try and get up there as soon as I can. Keep me in touch—and good luck. Hope it goes OK. Love you.'

He put the phone down and turned back to her with a smile. 'Sorry. That was Lucie, my sister. She's gone into labour. Mum's just going to drop her at the hospital, but she can't stay with her because of the boys.'

'And you want to go and take over from her, so she can be with Lucie?'

'No. I want to stay here with you, and make love to you again, but I have to live with myself,' he said with a wry grin, and she laughed softly and reached out a hand to touch him.

'You're such a good man,' she said, suddenly serious, and his smile died, his jaw working.

'No, I'm not,' he said quietly. 'If I was a good man I'd be looking forward to helping out, not doing it out of duty and wishing she'd had the sense to be careful and not have yet another unplanned pregnancy, another child she hasn't got the ability to provide for.' His hand trailed over her body, his fingers curling possessively over one breast, cupping it lovingly. 'So beautiful,' he murmured. 'I want to make love to you—want to hold you, and feel you, and listen to the frantic little noises that you make when you're getting closer...'

His mouth brushed hers, clung, and then she was in his arms again, their bodies striving, forging together as he drove her over the brink again, and with a ragged groan he stiffened, arching against her, his breath sobbing against her lips as he said her name over and over again.

He collapsed against her, rolling to the side

and taking her with him, stroking her back slowly, up and down, as his heartbeat slowed. 'I wasn't going to do that,' he said with an untidy sigh, and she laughed softly and pressed a tender kiss to his rough, stubbled chin.

'Don't worry, I won't tell,' she teased. 'Go and shower and shave. I'll make you some coffee and pack my things. You can give me a lift to the station in Ipswich and I'll pick up my car. You virtually pass it.'

'Good idea. Give me five minutes.'

He disappeared into the bathroom, and she slipped on his robe, pulled clean clothes out of her bag, repacked all her other things and put the bag by the door, then made them coffee and took hers out onto the deck to watch the sun rise.

It was only five, just four hours since they'd left the party, and they couldn't have slept more than three at the outside, probably less than that. By rights she should have felt hellish, but she didn't. She felt wonderful, vital and alive.

'You're a star,' he murmured behind her, and she turned to find him dressed only in jeans with the button undone, his coffee cupped in his hand and his eyes gentle. She wanted—desperately wanted—to go back into his arms, but that trail of dark hair arrowing down past that open button was threatening to undermine her self-control, so she just smiled.

'I know,' she said cheerfully, 'I'm fantastic. I'm just going to have a quick shower and get dressed, and I'll be with you. Why don't you eat something? I've put you in a slice of toast.'

And she went past him, somehow managing not to throw herself into his arms, and by the time she'd raced through the shower and pulled on her clothes, she was more or less back in control.

And at seven-thirty she was back home, and by ten he'd phoned to tell her that Lucie had had a girl and both of them were fine.

'So how are you?' she asked, and he gave a ragged laugh.

'Oh, I'm alive—just! The boys are a bit of a handful, but they're OK really. They just need a little direction, and frankly Lucie lets them get away with murder, so it's a bit of a struggle, but we've coped. Thanks for making me eat, by the way, because I really don't think I would have got round to it! Lucie's coming out this afternoon, apparently, and so I'm going to hang around here for the day, and then I might drop by and see you later if you're in.'

'Ring my mobile. I'm sure I won't be far. It'll be lovely to see you.'

But he didn't ring, not until much later, because Lucie's little girl developed a breathing problem and had to stay in, so she stayed with her and Nick took his mother and the boys to visit her, and it wasn't until the boys were finally in bed that he could get away to join her.

They went out for a drink to a pub on the seafront, and sat outside on a surprisingly warm evening for early May, and he told her all about the baby and what he and the boys had done that day.

'It sounds exhausting,' she said with a laugh, and he nodded, his answering grin a little crooked.

'It is. I could have done with more than two and a half hours' sleep. Still, she's OK now and they're hoping to come home in a day or two.'

'So what are you doing? Are you staying up here?'

'No. I've got meetings all day tomorrow, and Tuesday's a nightmare. I'm supposed to be going to Dublin. Mum can cope; the boys will be in school during the day so it's only the morning and evening, and she's pretty fit. She's only fifty-seven and she's well used to them.'

'Unlike you.'

'Unlike me,' he said with another crooked grin.

'So are you heading back to London now, or do you want to stay the night, or are you going to your mother's?'

He shook his head. 'Can't go to my mother's, she hasn't got room, and I really ought to get back ready for tomorrow. I start at six with a breakfast meeting.'

'Good grief! Well, I'd better not hold you up.'

'I wish you would. There's nothing I'd like more than to stay with you, but I can't get up at three-thirty and head back to London; I'm too darned tired. I need to get some decent sleep—and if I'm with you, I won't sleep, and if I'm in the room next to you, I won't sleep either, so I'm pretty much out of options!'

His smile was full of regret, and with a reluctant sigh he walked her back to the car and dropped her home, kissing her lingeringly.

'I'll see you in the week. I'll be up again to see them, and I'll come over. Maybe I'll stay then.'

'I'll look forward to it,' she said, but it never happened.

He didn't ring the next day, or the next, and on Wednesday when she gave in and called his phone, it was switched off. Her texts bounced, his home phone went straight to the answerphone, and when in desperation she phoned the office, she was told by someone whose voice she didn't recognise that Nick wasn't there and Tory was away from the office. No, she couldn't tell her where he was. No, she had no idea when he'd be back. Would she like to leave a message?

'Yes—it's Georgie Cauldwell, the architect for the Yoxburgh development. Can you ask him to call me as soon as you get hold of him, please?'

'Sure. I'll pass it on.'

And the line went dead.

So where was he, and where was Tory? Had she been wrong about Tory and Simon?

No. That was ridiculous. If ever a couple were falling in love, it was those two. She'd seen them together, seen the same look in Tory's eyes when she looked at Simon as she'd seen in her own reflection the morning after Nick had made love to her.

So if not with Tory, then where was he, and why hadn't he contacted her?

She tried him again later, then at midnight when she couldn't sleep, and again the following day.

Again, he wasn't there. It was a different receptionist this time, another voice she didn't recognise. Sorry, she had no idea when he'd be back. No, they couldn't get hold of him.

Damn. She'd been right all along. He wasn't really interested in her except for the novelty value, the thrill of the chase, and now he'd slept with her, the novelty had obviously worn off and he had better things to do.

She contemplated looking up his mother's number in the telephone directory—even got as far as taking the book off the shelf by the phone, but then she put it back, disgusted with herself for being so needy and pathetic. On Sunday afternoon, after another failed attempt, she went into the sitting room and dropped into the chair opposite her father with a sigh.

'Still can't get him?'

She shook her head, suddenly, perversely, on the verge of tears. 'I don't know where he is.'

'Have you tried the hospital? His sister's baby might be ill.'

Stupidly she hadn't even thought of it. She did it now, though, and was told that nobody by the name of Lucie Barron was in the hospital. 'We haven't got anyone with that name here,' the in-patient receptionist told her.

'She had a baby last Sunday morning,' Georgie told her, and was promptly transferred to Maternity.

'No, no one by that name at all recently,' she was told, and that was the end of that.

'She must have been married or had a different name for some reason,' Georgie told her father, going back into the sitting room and plopping into the chair again.

'He'll contact you. Something must have come up—you know how busy he is. Maybe he and Tory have had to fly to New York or Japan or something.'

'Probably,' she told herself, but she didn't believe it.

And then the following day she ran into a problem with the specification for the tower rooms in the house, and so she tried again.

'I'm sorry, I can't get him today. I'll pass your message on,' yet another receptionist said, and cut her off again.

Damn!

Well, if he was going to be that petty about it, she'd have to write to him and demand answers, because she wasn't going to be stonewalled by yet another would-be developer who wouldn't answer her questions!

She drafted a letter, tore it up and tried again, and then finally sent him an email asking him to contact her about the tower.

No begging, pleading or grovelling. No nasty remarks, no acid-drops or smart comments.

She even managed to stop herself from signing off with, 'love, Georgie'.

And then the following morning, nine days after she'd last seen him, she was up in the tower when an unfamiliar estate car pulled up outside the site office. She peered at it, rubbed the dust off the window with her sleeve and blinked.

'Nick?'

No. She was seeing things.

No, she wasn't. She ran down the stairs and forced herself to walk to the car. He had the back door open and was talking to someone, and as she drew nearer he straightened up and turned towards her.

He was wearing a suit—a black suit, with a white shirt and a black tie. Good grief, talk about over-dressed. He looks as if he's going to a funeral, she thought, and then she saw his face.

'Nick? Nick, whatever's happened?' Her voice was little more than a whisper, and for a moment he couldn't speak, just swallowed, his throat working furiously.

Then he lifted his tortured eyes to hers.

'There was an accident, on the way home from the hospital. Mum's injured, and Lucie—' He broke off, a muscle in his jaw jumping, then said, 'Lucie...'

CHAPTER FIVE

HE COULDN'T finish the sentence. He didn't need to. His clothes said it all. She looked into the back of the car and met two pairs of wary, frightened eyes, and her heart contracted.

And there between them was a rear-facing baby seat, the only visible evidence of its occupant a tiny, waving fist.

Her hand came up to cover her mouth, to hold back the cry of denial, but there was no denying it. It was in his eyes, the grief, the despair, the utter disbelief.

'Oh, Nick—why didn't you ring me?'

'I tried. I couldn't finish dialling your number. I didn't know what to say.'

'You could have sent me a text. I would have come to you, helped you. You didn't have to do this alone.'

'I didn't. I've got Tory, but I need a favour, Georgie. I need you to help me. I'd got the funeral covered but they hate the nanny and she's walked out. Can you—? I'm sorry, but I can't have them there. They're too young, and my mother—'

'It's all right,' she said, moving to hug him, but he backed away, his hands rammed in his pockets.

'Don't touch me, Georgie. Don't be nice to me, for God's sake. I'm hanging by a thread.'

Her hands fell to her sides and she nodded, biting her lip to hold back the words that would push him over the edge.

'So,' she said after a moment, then cleared her throat and tried again. 'What do you want me to do?'

'Can I follow you home and leave the kids there with you? It shouldn't be too long—four hours or so? Shut the site down if you have to; I'll pay their wages. I wouldn't do this to you if I could avoid it, but Mum's just distraught and I have to collect her from the hospital and take her to the funeral, then take her back. I can't subject the kids to that and I don't know who else to turn to.'

'No, of course you can't. It's fine. Give me ten seconds to programme Andy, and I'll be with you.'

She turned on her heel and ran over to the coach house where Andy was working, filled him in and then ran to her car, flashing her lights at Nick as she started it up and pulled out in front of him. He fell in behind her, trailed her to her house and there he got the children out while she hurried in and warned her father, then went back out to help him with the little ones.

'Kids, this is Georgie,' he said, the baby in her carrier in one hand, his other hand rested on the small, tousled head of the younger boy. 'She's going to look after you today. Georgie, this is Dickon, and his big brother, Harry, and the baby's called Maya.' Harry stood a fraction apart, isolated in his loss, his eyes wary, and Georgie could have wept.

Oh, good grief, she thought, they're so young—too young to have lost their mother. Especially the baby. She'll never know her— never have any memories—

Stop! She sucked in a deep breath and smiled at them. 'Hello, boys. Come on inside and meet my father, and we'll see if we can find you something to eat and drink, OK?'

'Have you got biscuits?' Dickon asked, but Harry turned to Nick, his eyes fathoms deep.

'I want to stay with you. I won't be a nuisance.'

Nick's face contorted for a moment, and he reached out, drawing Harry against his side and hugging him briefly. 'Sorry, Harry. No can do. I have to go and fetch Grandma and take her to the funeral and then take her back, but you could look after Dickon and Maya for me while I'm gone—give Georgie a hand.'

She saw the boy withdraw into himself as he nodded and detached himself reluctantly from his uncle's side.

Nick handed her the baby in her reclining seat, then reached into the car for a bulging bag, his eyes bleak. 'This should see her through. It's got nappies and formula and bottles and a couple of changes of clothes and a blanket and probably the kitchen sink as well. I don't know. I expect I've forgotten something vital, but I hope not. If I have, just buy whatever you need and I'll sort it out with you later. And here's the buggy, in case you want to go for a walk. The seat clips into it. If you get stuck—'

'We'll be fine,' she told him, staring down at the tiny sleeping baby and wondering how fate could possibly be so cruel. She sucked in a deep breath and turned, to find her father in the doorway, his kindly face creased with concern.

'Hello, boys,' he said gently. 'Come on inside and we'll see if we can find those biscuits. Georgie can bring the baby. Nick.'

Just the one word, but conveying a world of concern and support, and Nick nodded acknowledgement and stared hard at the ground for a moment. The boys trailed in, Harry looking over his shoulder, and Nick gave him the ghost of a wink in support and turned back to Georgie. 'Um—I ought to be getting off. Don't want to be late.'

'No. You go, we'll cope. We'll see you whenever.'

'Thanks.'

'Not necessary. Go on.'

He hesitated for a second, then got into the car and drove away, and she picked up the baby and turned towards the door, to find Harry standing there looking after his uncle with those bottomless eyes.

'Come on,' she said gently, placing a hand

lightly on his shoulder and steering him back inside, closing the door behind them. She could hear Dickon and her father in the kitchen, and she ushered Harry in there and introduced him to Archie, who was busy washing Dickon's face.

Now, she thought, was probably not the time to point out that it wasn't a good idea, and anyway, on balance it was probably just what the little boy needed. It would probably do Nick a power of good, too, but he was out of her hands for the moment and the baby was waking up.

'Harry, do you know what time Maya was fed?' she asked, but Harry shook his head.

'Just feed her. If she isn't hungry, she won't have it,' he said logically, and Georgie could have hugged him for that injection of common sense into this fraught and difficult situation.

'Want to give me a hand? I'm not too great with babies.'

He gave a careless shrug, and started to look in the bag. 'Here—you have to heat it in the microwave for one minute and give it a shake and check it on your arm. It mustn't be too hot or it'll burn her mouth.'

So much wisdom. He must have been all of six years old. He handed her the bottle—tiny, to suit the tiny baby—and she heated and tested it as instructed, while her father and Dickon were making drinks and putting a ridiculous number of biscuits out on a plate, to make a pattern.

Well, Dickon was making the pattern. Her father was watching, his brow furrowed and his lips pressed together firmly, as if he was struggling. Georgie could understand that. She was struggling too, the now suckling baby snuggled against her breast, tiny starfish hands clutching the bottle and kneading rhythmically.

It should have been her mother's breast, she thought sadly. Oh, little one, what have you lost? What have you all lost? And what will become of you?

She looked up, to find that Harry and Dickon

were settled at the table with her father, deep in conversation about diggers. Well, her father and Dickon were, and Harry was listening, but Georgie guessed it would take a little longer to draw him out.

'You have to burp her,' Harry said, and she realised she had no idea how to burp a baby. Oh, she'd seen it done, but she'd never really taken the slightest bit of notice—

'Here, let me do it,' her father said, and, taking Maya from her, he sat down again, settled her on his knee and with his big, thick fingers cupping her chin he placed his other hand gently on her back and rubbed, slowly and rhythmically, until the baby obliged with a deafening burp that made them all laugh, even Harry.

It was easier after that. Harry found a nappy and the changing mat and showed Georgie how to change her nappy, and she marvelled at this little boy, so self-possessed. How was he

dealing with the loss of his mother? It didn't
bear thinking about.

'You're a star,' she said and hugged him, and
for the briefest moment he clung to her, then
got to his feet and went over to the window.

'Do you think Nick will be long?' he asked,
his gaze fixed on the drive.

She met her father's eyes. 'Some time longer,
I think,' she said cautiously.

'I wanted to go to the funeral. We saw a
funeral in India—they put flowers in the river
so they'd float away. It was pretty.'

'Will they do that with Mummy?' Dickon
asked, looking up from rearranging the remain-
ing biscuits. 'Float her away in a river?'

'No. They're going to dig a hole and put her
in, and they're going to plant a tree on her.
Grandma said she was worth more than a cardboard box, and she cried. I heard Uncle Nick
telling Tory,' he added, answering Georgie's
unspoken question. 'But he said Mummy

wanted that, and so she should have it. Are we staying here for lunch?'

'Oh, I expect so,' Georgie said, heaving a sigh of relief that the conversation had moved on. 'What would you like?'

'Bacon sandwiches. Mummy's vegetarian, but we like bacon sandwiches, don't we?'

Dickon nodded. 'Uncle Nick gives them to us all the time. And triple-choc-chunk cookies. They're yummy.'

And not a portion of fruit and veg in sight, Georgie thought, but decided the day of their mother's funeral wasn't the day to worry about that, and anyway, she was only babysitting them briefly.

'We haven't got any bacon,' her father said, his brow puckered.

'No, but we could go for a walk. It's a lovely day, and I know just the place for a bacon sandwich. And they sell ice cream, and you can play on the beach for a while if you like.' She looked at her father. 'Are you feeling up to it?'

He nodded. 'Sure. I've got to have my walk today anyway, so a little trip down to the beach sounds like fun. I can always lean on the baby's buggy.'

'What if Uncle Nick comes back?' Harry said, his insecurity showing again, but Georgie patted her mobile phone in her pocket.

'He can get me any time. He knows my number. Fancy it?'

They nodded. 'Can we go in the sea?' Dickon asked, but George shook his head firmly.

'No. It won't be warm enough yet. But you can play on the sand. Georgie, can you find that old bucket and spade?'

And so, a few minutes later, equipped with a bucket and spade that she remembered from her childhood, and the old striped windbreak, they set off, Georgie pushing the baby in her buggy with the emergency kit stashed under the seat and her father leading the way, a small boy attached to the end of each arm as they straggled down to the beach.

Harry had Archie on his lead, and for once the little dog was behaving as if he'd seen the inside of a training class, trotting along beside Harry as if he'd been doing it for years.

'Lunch first?' she suggested as they reached the café on the prom, and with Archie tied up outside they squeezed up to the end by the window, the buggy with a sleeping Maya tucked into the corner and the boys squabbling over the menu until Georgie took it away from them.

'I thought you wanted bacon sandwiches?' she said.

'But we need a drink,' Dickon said with his wide, guileless eyes, and she met her father's eyes and smiled.

'How about a milkshake? I think they do strawberry or chocolate.'

'Chocolate,' Dickon said promptly, and Harry frowned at him.

'I wanted chocolate.'

'But I said it first—'

'You can both have chocolate, it's not a problem,' Georgie said, cutting off the argument. 'Do you want squirty cream on the top?'

They did, of course, and fidgeted until the drinks came, then just as the sandwiches arrived the baby woke and started to cry, and Georgie had to ask for the bottle to be heated, and then it was too hot, and then Maya's nappy needed changing, and by the time she'd come back from doing that her coffee was stone cold, her bacon sandwich was starting to congeal, the boys were getting restless and she was wondering how long it would be before Nick came and took them away.

Too long, she thought, eating the sandwich anyway because as usual she'd skipped breakfast and was starving. She couldn't cope with this. No. That was rubbish. Of course she could cope. She just didn't want to have to.

'Can we go now?' Dickon asked, the moment the last morsel went into her mouth, and, laughing at his impatience, she drained the dregs of her coffee, pulled a face and stood up.

'Come on, then. Let's go and hit the beach.'

And her father sat on the sand with the baby on his lap, trying to bring up her wind while Georgie built sandcastles with the boys and taught them how to skim pebbles and wondered how Nick was getting on.

'Nice having children round again,' her father said later, as she sat beside him watching the boys building a fort while Archie dug a huge hole beside them.

'Don't. I'm not getting involved with these kids, Dad. I can't do that again.'

'I wonder what he'll do about them?'

She'd been wondering the same thing herself,

but hadn't come up with anything sensible. After all, he was a man, a bachelor, with a bachelor lifestyle to match, and she couldn't imagine the kids in his Dockland apartment any more than she could picture him living in suburbia with two-point-four children.

And the point-four chose that moment to screw up her little face and strain, and Georgie's heart sank. Another nappy. They only had one left, and she had no idea when Nick would get back.

'We ought to walk home through the town and pick up some stuff for the baby,' she said to her father. 'She's running out of nappies, and she's only got one more feed in the bag. If he gets held up…'

So they rounded up the tired but reluctant children, put the dog back on his lead and headed up the beach towards the building site just above them on the other side of the road.

'It's looking good,' her father said, tipping

back his head and admiring the renovated house with its new slate roof, crisp white windows with their gleaming panes, its freshly painted walls glowing pale cream in the afternoon sun. 'You've done a great job.'

She warmed to his praise, but there was still a lingering disappointment. 'I wanted that tower,' she said wistfully, and her father shot her an odd look.

'You might get it yet.'

'I don't think so. Especially not if the equation has just shifted to take in the two-point-four.'

George looked down at the children and smiled wryly. 'You never know, you might get used to it—'

'Dad, no. Please don't start. I know you miss Jessica and Emily, but I can't do it again, and anyway, it might not even be on the cards. It's far too soon in all sorts of ways. Don't go jumping the gun.'

'We'll see,' was all he'd say, and he held out

his hands and called the boys, and they ran to him, tucking their little hands in his and chattering non-stop all the way to the shops, their earlier reticence now gone. They picked up a few bits from the little supermarket for the baby, and then made their way home, by which time they were all looking weary, her father particularly.

'Why don't you three sit down and find something on the television to watch, and I'll make us all something to eat?' she suggested, and to her surprise the boys didn't even put up a token protest, but snuggled up on George's lap, one each side tucked into the crook of an arm, and they settled down to watch the children's programmes while she took the baby in the kitchen, fed her again, bathed her a little nervously in the sink and then dressed her in fresh clothes and settled her down in the buggy for a nap.

It was four-thirty. Hours after she'd expected Nick to return, and there'd been no word from him. She looked down at the baby, so tiny, so defenceless and helpless, and felt a wave of overwhelming sadness.

How would her grandmother be coping? Nick had said very little about her injuries, but they were obviously severe enough to keep her in hospital for more than a week, and on top of that she had to cope with the loss of her daughter and the worry about what would happen to the children. From what Nick had said there wasn't anyone else to take care of them, not one of the fathers on the scene, and with his mother out of action, who did that leave?

Nick.

She swallowed the sickening wave of disappointment.

No. They were getting on so well, or they had been, and she'd begun to believe that things might even develop into something serious.

Not this serious, though. Not in a million

years. But maybe it would only be temporary, until his mother was better.

Suddenly needing to be busy, she scoured the fridge and cupboards for something the children would eat and that would keep so she could offer some to Nick when he turned up, and found a jar of Stroganoff sauce and a few frozen chicken breasts.

Onions in the sauce? The children might not eat them, she thought, and then remembered that Lucie had been a vegetarian. Should she give the children chicken and go against their mother's principles? What about the bacon, come to that? It was a bit late to worry about Lucie's principles.

She looked again. Mushrooms, peppers, courgettes, carrots—she could do a vegetarian version for the children if necessary. She'd ask them, she decided, and put her head round the sitting-room door to find that they were all fast asleep—her father, his head lolling and a soft snore coming from him, with the dog out cold at his feet and the boys likewise, Harry cuddled into him, Dickon sprawled on his back, mouth open, looking far too small to be an orphan—

No. Stop thinking about it. And of course it doesn't matter if they eat chicken. What they need is love and food and for today, at least, they'd get it. What happened after that would take care of itself, and she wouldn't be a part of it.

She heard the scrunch of tyres on the drive, and went to the door, opening it just as Nick cut the engine and sat there, his eyes meeting hers through the windscreen.

He looks awful, she thought as he climbed out of the car and walked heavily towards her.

'How are they?' he asked.

'Fine. They're sleeping. We went to the beach.'

His shoulders dropped a fraction with the release of tension. 'I was worried about you all.'

'No need, we've been fine. How about you?'

'Dreadful. I didn't think Mum would get through it—'

His voice cracked, and she looked at him searchingly. He was still holding it all together, she realised, hanging on, doing everything for everybody else and not thinking about himself.

'Come in a moment,' she said, and drew him inside, putting a finger to her lips and showing him the boys asleep on her father. His eyes were open now, and George smiled at Nick and looked down fondly at the boys.

'Busy day,' he mouthed, and Nick nodded.

'Can you cope for half an hour?' Georgie said softly, and he nodded assent.

'Baby all right?' he whispered.

'Just fed her and put her down.'

He nodded again, and, leaving the door open so he could listen out for Maya, she led Nick back outside, put him in her car and drove him to the now deserted building site.

'What are we doing?' he asked as she cut the engine outside the site and unlocked the gates, then opened his door.

'What nobody else has done yet—given you time out. Come on.'

She took him by the hand, led him into the site hut and shut the door, then put her arms round him and hugged him.

'Georgie, no…' he protested, but she could feel the tension vibrating in his chest, the ragged breathing, the pain all lined up waiting for a chance to be freed if he'd only let go.

'Yes. You need a hug. You look awful,' she murmured, cupping his cheek gently. 'Was it dreadful today?'

He nodded, swallowing hard. 'It was such a lovely day, it just seemed all wrong—'

He broke off, his jaw working, and she slipped her arms round him again and hugged him gently. 'I'm so sorry,' she said, and she felt his ribs heave under her hands. He moved away from her, turning to look out of the window with sightless eyes.

'She was such a crazy girl. A real one-off.

She was my baby sister, Georgie. I just can't believe she's gone—'

And that was it. His shoulders heaved, and she turned him back into her arms, holding him fiercely as the wave of grief tore through him and left him spent and exhausted in her arms. Finally he lifted his head and stared at the ceiling, sniffing hard and letting out a ragged breath.

'I'm sorry.'

'Don't be. That's why I brought you here, so you could get it out of your system out of earshot of the children.'

He rummaged in his pocket for a tissue, still immaculately folded and untouched even after his hellish day, and while he mopped himself up she put the kettle on and found some clean mugs.

'Tell me about it,' she said, and he dropped into a chair and stared sightlessly at the floor.

'There were so many people there,' he said wonderingly. 'Friends of Mum's and Lucie's, old school friends—I got hold of Lucie's address book and gave it to Tory. She did a bit of a ring-round and they passed it on and everybody came. It was a green burial—Mum hated it, but it was what Lucie had always talked about, and really it was beautiful. I think Mum would have hated it whatever, just because it shouldn't have been happening.'

'The boys were talking about it—what would happen at the funeral. They heard you talking to Tory about the coffin and your mother's reaction.'

His head jerked up and his eyes met hers. 'Really? Damn. What did they say?'

'Just that she thought Lucie was worth more than a cardboard box. They were talking about funerals in India and planting a tree on her and things like that. All very matter-of-fact—I don't think they really understand.'

'I don't know. Harry might. Dickon's much more accepting, but he's asked me when his mummy's coming home and I don't know how to tell him…'

His face contorted again, and he looked away, cleared his throat and apologised.

'Don't be silly. You don't need to pretend with me, or hold it together. I know what grief's like, I've done it. Tea or coffee?'

'Brandy?' he said wryly, and she smiled.

'We've got some at home. Do you want to stay the night?'

He stared at her. 'Do you mind? I'm just exhausted. Tory's gone back to London to try and sort out the chaos in the office—the receptionist's been off sick and we've had temps in.'

'I know. I've left messages with three different people in the past few days.'

'Oh, Georgie, I'm sorry. I didn't get any of them. I should have rung you, but I was afraid if I saw you or spoke to you I wouldn't be able to hold it together, and I had so much to do—'

'It's OK. I understand. I can remember what it's like.' Then she took a deep breath and voiced the question that had been troubling her all day, ever since he'd arrived that morning with the children in tow and left them with her.

'So—what happens next? Are you going to take the children back to London?'

He shook his head. 'How can I? My apartment isn't exactly set up for kids. I can just see the boys falling over the railings off the deck and the baby drowning in the hot tub.'

'It'll be a while before she can get in it,' Georgie pointed out, and he gave her a strained smile.

'I know, but you know what I mean. They can't live there, it's not the right environment for children, and Mum's cottage is far too small. We'll need a house that's big enough for Mum and the kids and a nanny, that will give Mum a studio for her art and room for me to come and stay at weekends.'

In London, she realised. One of the nicer residential areas, close enough to commute to his office, far enough out to be civilised. And with him light-years from being the bachelor playboy she'd fallen for so hard and so fast. Still, he'd be safely out of the way, and she'd get over him in time, she thought, and then he dropped the bombshell.

'In fact, it occurred to me that I've already got one, if we can change things yet again.'

Georgie followed his eyes, looking through the window to the big house sitting just a hundred yards away, and her heart lurched.

'Here?' she said incredulously.

'Why not? It's a fabulous house, it's in a lovely setting, it's near to my mother's friends—what could be better?'

You somewhere else, miles away, not right here under my nose tearing my heart out with those beautiful little children until you get bored with me and move on—

'Nothing,' she said, honesty forcing her to admit the truth. 'It's perfect.'

And she'd just have to keep her heart firmly under control.

CHAPTER SIX

'How soon can you do it?'

Georgie shrugged. 'Three weeks?'

'One? It doesn't have to be finished—just enough to get us moved in. All we need at first is a kitchen and a bathroom and the main rooms—sitting room, three or four bedrooms?'

One week? He was crazy. She took a sip of her wine, stared down at the plans again and made a few pencilled annotations.

Her father had gone to bed, the children had been tucked up hours ago after eating the chicken Stroganoff that Nick had sanctioned, and they were hunched over the plans on the kitchen table and trying to get a workable solution for his complex needs. And boy, were they complex!

She'd learned a little more about the accident, as well. The car had been hit in the side by a vehicle coming out of a side-turning without looking, and both the driver and Lucie had been killed instantly. The boys and the baby had escaped miraculously without injury, but as well as a badly bruised breast-bone, Nick's mother's lower right leg had been shattered and she had a fixator on it, a metal frame on the outside holding the bones in place. Even thinking about it made Georgie feel queasy. Nick told her it would be another week before she was able to leave hospital, and then she'd need a place to go where she could have a bathroom and bedroom on the ground floor so she could get about on crutches.

And that was possible now, with the plans as they were, but if the entire house was to be turned back into one unit and adapted for their future needs, then the bathroom that was in the process of being installed would need to be moved to another room. It was so easy on the computer—just click on it, and drag and drop, but try telling the plumber that!

'Georgie?'

She looked up from the plans into his sad, exhausted eyes and pushed herself away from the table.

'I'll do what I can. Come on, you're done in. You need to get to bed. I've put you in the spare room where you were before.'

'What about the baby?'

'I've got her in with me, just for tonight.'

'Georgie, that's not fair—'

'Nick, none of this is fair, but you're wiped and this could go on for ages. You need your sleep, so you might as well have one decent night.'

He opened his mouth as if to argue, shut it again and pulled her into his arms.

'Thank you,' he mumbled into her hair. 'I've missed you.'

'I've missed you, too. I thought you were ignoring my calls because you'd gone off me.'

He laughed and hugged her tighter. 'Not a chance. I'm sorry. I wish I'd rung you now, but I just couldn't bring myself to say it. Anyway, it won't be like this for long. Once I get a new nanny sorted in the morning and the house is up and running, I should be able to get back to normal. I'm going to have to be more involved in their lives than I have been, but I'm sure we'll all cope.'

He made it sound so easy. So do-able. She hugged him back, snuggling against his chest and wishing they could spend the night together, but with the children in the house it didn't seem right.

Still, as he'd said, it wouldn't be long. He'd have a nanny in the next couple of days, and then they could get back to normal.

* * *

'What do you mean, you haven't got anyone? You must have!'

He listened to the reasonable explanations of the woman at the nanny agency, then hung up with a growl and tried another one. Same story. Nobody suitable.

He rang Tory. 'Find me a nanny,' he barked, and after a pointed silence he added, 'please.'

'I'll do what I can. How are things?'

Frustrating. 'Fine,' he lied. 'Georgie's going to try and have the house sorted in the next few days. In the meantime I don't know what to do. We spent last night with her and her father, but we can't impose on them again, and the cottage…'

'Is full of Lucie's things,' Tory finished gently.

He swallowed hard. 'Silly, isn't it? Maybe we should just check into a hotel.'

He heard a noise behind him and turned, to find Georgie standing there in the doorway. He smiled at her and held up his hand to stop her going away. 'Tory, if you could just sort the nanny thing for me that would be great. Any time in the next half-hour will do.'

'You have no idea how big a Christmas bonus you're going to give me,' she said, but there was a smile in her voice and he laughed softly as she put the phone down on him. He turned back to Georgie, the smile still hovering, but she was biting her lip in that way she had when things were troubling her, and he gave up with the smile and held out his hand to her.

'What is it?'

She went over, letting him pull her up against his side. 'You don't have to go to a hotel,' she said. 'You can all stay here. There's tons of room, and Dad's really enjoying having the children around.'

He tipped his head back and studied her face searchingly. 'What about you? Are you enjoying having them around?'

She shrugged. 'What about me? I'm busy at work. It doesn't matter about me.'

'So you don't want them here.'

'I didn't say that,' she protested, pulling away, and he let her go and stood up and followed her out of the kitchen and into George's office by the front door. He wasn't letting this one drop.

'It's what you meant.'

'No.'

He wasn't convinced, but he changed the subject—for now. 'Were you coming to see me about something?'

'Mmm—the house. I've done some plans— want to see?'

He nodded, and she pulled out a chair for him at the desk, bringing up the plans on the computer and pointing to the changes.

'If we move the bathroom to here, and put a doorway here into this bit, these could be your mother's permanent rooms. If we gave her this room as her sitting room, she could have access to the conservatory when we rebuild it…'

Why couldn't he concentrate? This was important—vital, in fact—but somehow it couldn't compete with the fresh citrus smell of shampoo drifting from her hair and the way her lips moved as she was talking, the quick little darts of her hand as she pointed things out to him.

'So what do you think? Does she need her own kitchen?'

He sucked in a deep breath, ignored the fresh wave of citrus that assailed his senses and stared at the plans. 'Run it by me again?'

He couldn't get a nanny. He'd been on the phone all day trying to sort it out, and every time she'd tried to ring him to ask for his input, his phone had been engaged. Tory had been driven insane by him, Georgie was sure, but still there was no nanny in the pipeline, and the business was beginning to clamour for his attention.

He was getting desperate, she could see. He came off the phone to Tory yet again and threw his mobile on the desk in disgust, just as she came through to her father's office with a cup of tea for him.

'Problems?'

'Georgie, I've got to get back to London. The business will be going down the tubes.'

'Can't Tory keep you in touch?'

He sighed and scrubbed his hands through his hair for the umpteenth time. 'She is—well, she's trying, but it's impossible without appropriate internet connections.'

Her heart was howling in protest, her head was busy saying no as loud as it could, but her mouth seemed to have a mind of its own.

'We've got broadband. Go down to London, get whatever computer stuff you need, I'll clear you a space in the office and you can get yourself back here by the morning and sort it out.'

'What about the kids?'

Oh, hell. She was getting sucked in deeper and deeper, but what else could she do? 'I'll look after them,' she told him. 'Just so long as you really have torn up that penalty clause.'

He grinned and hugged her. 'Absolutely. No penalty clause—and I'll be back first thing. If you're really sure?'

'I'm sure. Go on, say goodbye to the kids and get yourself back here as soon as you reasonably can.'

'I will. With a nanny, if possible.'

'I won't hold my breath,' she said drily, and wondered what on earth she was doing...

He came back at seven the next morning, but there was still no nanny. Nevertheless she left the children with him with a clear conscience, went to the site and made herself a cup of tea before settling down in front of her desk and studying her list of queries.

The plumber was going to walk off site, she

thought, and good for him. She felt like doing it herself, because she knew perfectly well that if she stayed she'd become massively involved with the whole family. Her father already adored the children, he thought the world of Nick, and all Georgie could think of was Martin and how he'd returned the children to their mother and walked away from her without a backward glance.

Not that she'd cared about him, not really. She'd grown up a lot during the course of their relationship, realised he was only using her, but she'd thought she had the children, couldn't have loved them more if they'd been her own, and she could see it happening all over again.

Not handing them back to their mother, of course, because tragically that would never be an option, but loving them would be so easy. *Was* so easy. The boys were gorgeous, and holding the baby just seemed so right, so natural, that at times she was almost surprised that she couldn't breast-feed her. Bizarre. And much, much too dangerous for her heart.

She stared at her list and sighed. First step was to find the plumber and break the good news…

It was a miracle! Tory had found him a nanny— a tall, pretty Swedish girl called Una, with a stunning figure and hair to die for. Under any other circumstances Georgie would have hated her on sight, but she greeted her arrival with a huge sigh of relief, changed the sheets on her bed and relinquished it and the baby without a qualm.

Well, almost. The bed Una was welcome to. The baby was different, and when she woke in the night Georgie woke too, listening to Una's gentle murmurings and the baby's quiet grizzling until her bottle was prepared.

Then silence, and Georgie gave up her vigil at the top of the attic stairs and tiptoed back to bed, calling herself an idiot. Una was perfectly capable of looking after the baby—much more capable, in fact, than Georgie herself, and she didn't need watching over like a rookie plasterer let loose on a ballroom ceiling!

She curled up in bed, pulled the sheets over her head and ignored the cries when they started. Una could cope. Una would be fine. Una didn't need her help…

'Can I do anything?'

Una looked up from her seat in the middle of the sofa and smiled bravely. 'I can manage,' she said, but Maya was protesting, and Georgie's arms ached.

'Let me try. Sometimes she just needs a little jiggle to bring up her wind.'

And, resting the baby over her shoulder as if she'd been doing it for years, Georgie walked slowly up and down the floor, jiggling gently, until at last the baby burped, sighed and snuggled against her, tiny face rooting against her neck. 'Here,' she said, handing the baby back. 'She'll be fine now.'

And she trudged resolutely up the stairs, ignoring the faint whimpering from behind her. She turned the corner to the attic stairs and found Harry sitting on the bottom step, his eyes wet.

'Hey, sport,' she said softly, and sat beside him. 'You OK?'

'I had a dream. We were in the car, and there was a great big bang, and when I woke up the baby was crying. It was horrid.'

Oh, poor lamb. How on earth could he deal with this?

There was another wail from Maya, and Harry sighed. 'She needs her mummy,' he said, and Georgie knew he wasn't just talking about the baby, but about all of them.

She slipped her arm around his skinny little shoulders and hugged him gently. 'Want to sleep with me tonight?'

He nodded, and, taking his hand, she led him up to the attic room she was using, climbed into bed and held up the covers for him to slip in beside her. He snuggled into her arms, and gradually the tension left his little body and he relaxed into sleep.

Georgie didn't. She listened for Maya and Dickon, and she watched over Harry, until the dawn broke in the sky outside her bedroom window and the demons of the night were driven away. Then, and only then, did she allow herself to sleep.

Nick was beside himself.

There was no sign of Harry, and in desperation he ran up to Georgie to ask if she'd seen him, and found them curled up together in her bed, sound asleep. Weak with relief, he sagged against the wall and watched them sleep, while his heart slowed and his breathing returned to normal.

This was crazy. The sooner his mother was out of hospital and able to cope with Una's help, the sooner he could get back to London and start living a normal life, because this was doing his head in. It was so long since he'd had to take responsibility for anyone or anything other than himself and his own affairs that he'd forgotten how—if he'd ever known.

He thought it unlikely that he had. And what he knew about raising children could be written on the head of a pin.

In capitals.

He sighed, scrubbed his hand through his hair and looked up to find Georgie's eyes on him.

'Morning,' she murmured, and he had an insane urge to pick Harry up and return him to his own bed and take his place there with Georgie. Her face was flushed and her eyes were soft with sleep, and she looked unutterably lovely and unbelievably sexy.

He went over to the bed, resisted the urge to pick Harry up and evict him, and bent over, dropping a soft, lingering kiss on her lips.

'Morning,' he murmured back. 'That looks really inviting.'

She smiled, her eyes smoky and incredibly tempting, and he backed away before he did anything stupid.

'I'd invite you to join in, but I think three might be a crowd.'

'I think so,' he replied, his voice sounding a little strangled to his desperate ears, and he headed for the door. 'I'll put the kettle on— make you a cup of tea.'

'Thanks. I'll be down in a minute.'

He escaped without disgracing himself, retrieved a dressing gown to give his irrepressible libido another layer of camouflage and went down to the kitchen, to find George in there with the kettle in his hand.

'Everyone all right?'

'Mmm. Harry must have woken in the night. He's in bed with Georgie.'

'Is he indeed?' George murmured softly. 'I

didn't think it would take long. She protests a lot, but she loves kids. She got hurt last time, though, and it's made her wary.'

'Last time?'

George sent him a searching look. 'She not told you about Jessica and Emily? Martin's two?'

Martin. That was the name of her boss, if he remembered correctly. What was it she'd said about him? He'd had marital problems and brought them to her—them, meaning his girls?

'Not in detail,' he said, bending the truth for the sake of extracting more information from George.

'Ah, well, you'd better have it from her. Suffice to say when it all ended it broke her heart, purely on account of the children. Nothing to do with him, I don't think. He was a louse, and she was far too good for him, and I think she realised it by the end. I was glad to see the back of him, but I miss the girls. It's nice to have children in the house again, even if it is just for a short while.'

'Hopefully,' he agreed. 'Georgie's doing a fantastic job with the house. I don't think it'll be many days now. The carpets are due to go down tomorrow, I think, and the new bathroom's underway. Another two days and it can be done, and then we could move in.'

'You don't have to be in such a hurry, you know,' George said quietly. 'If you need another few days…'

'Thanks, but my mother's due to come out of hospital after the weekend and I think we need to get her settled straight away. I'll have to go over to the cottage and get some of her things, and I need to get more stuff for the children.'

Did his reluctance show, or was George just very perceptive? Whatever, he said, 'Why don't you go over with Georgie one evening and sort it out? You could get everything ready and then get a firm to pick it up.'

'What about the children?' he said. 'I don't

want to upset them—all their mother's things are there, and I don't feel ready to deal with it.'

'Leave them here. Between me and Una, we can cope.'

And he wouldn't have to face it alone. Until that moment he hadn't really realised how much he was dreading it, and now he felt as if a great weight had been lifted from his shoulders.

'Thanks,' he said gruffly.

George gave him an awkward pat on the shoulder. 'Don't mention it,' he said, equally gruffly, and thrust a mug in his hand. 'Here, wrap yourself round that.'

'I promised Georgie a cup.'

'She'll be down. There's more in the pot. Sit down and tell me how your mother's doing.'

She was going to kill her father.

She stood outside the kitchen, her silent approach in bare feet having got her to this point just as they were discussing her relation-ship with Martin.

Why? she thought. Why did you have to tell him everything?

Although to be fair he hadn't told Nick every-thing, exactly, but it was enough, and now he was volunteering her to help him retrieve things from his mother's house. Well, she didn't mind that, she conceded, but she could have been consulted first.

Creeping up the first few stairs, she turned and ran down, walked through the kitchen door with a cheery smile and headed for the teapot. If her father was really, really lucky, she wouldn't break it over his head!

'Thanks for helping me.'

She gave him a wry smile. 'You're welcome,' she said, and he was. He truly was, despite her reaction at the time, and she could see how hard it would have been for him on his own.

As it was they'd gone through the house, retrieved all Lucie's things and put them together
in the little bedroom she'd shared with the boys.
Their things were packed and loaded into his
car, and a selection of his mother's things had
been assembled in boxes in the sitting room
and bedroom, together with certain items of
furniture that had been labelled and listed ready
for the removal firm who were due to come in
the morning.

They drove back the twenty miles from
Framlingham to Yoxburgh, and as they entered
the town he turned not right, towards her father's
house, but left, heading down to the site.

'What are you doing?' she asked.

'Got your site keys?'

'I always have the site keys,' she replied.
'Why?'

'Because it's a beautiful night, and I want to go
up in the tower with you and look at the moonlight on the sea, and just be alone with you.'

Her heart bumped against her ribs. She didn't reply, just slipped her hand over his on the steering wheel and squeezed gently.

It was enough. She unlocked the house, and he took her by the hand and led her up the carpeted stairs to the room at the top, and there he took her in his arms and made love to her in the moonlight. Afterwards they sat on the window sill, staring out over the smooth, lazy swell of the sea, their fingers entwined.

'I love you,' he said softly.

Her fingers tightened on his. 'I love you, too,' her mouth said, her heart joining in despite the desperate protests from her feeble mind. Oh, damn, why had she said that?

He pulled her into his arms and hugged her. 'I couldn't have got through tonight without you. Thank you for being there for me.'

'You're welcome,' she said, and wondered how long it would be before she came to regret those three little words that she'd never meant to say.

CHAPTER SEVEN

THE tower room became their favourite place.

Every day he came over to see how things were going in the house, and after they'd looked round it they'd end their tour in the top of the tower.

He'd decided to have it as another little sitting room cum home office, and Georgie couldn't wait to see it finished. He'd ordered the most fabulous furniture for the bedrooms that were completed, and for the main sitting room, and also for the tower room.

It was going to be wonderful, as she'd always known it would, and although it would never be hers, that didn't stop her from loving it. She escaped to it whenever she could steal a minute, and so did Nick.

They went there several times over the weekend, snatching an hour here, half an hour there, sometimes making love but often just to sit and be alone together with the ever-changing sea stretched out below them as far as they could see. And they talked about Lucie, and Georgie built up a picture of her that just made the children's loss even more poignant.

'It'll be nice to have some furniture,' he said on Sunday evening, lying propped up against the wall with Georgie in his arms watching the clouds scud across the sky.

She laughed. 'I would have suggested thicker underlay if I'd realised we'd spend so much time sitting on it,' she teased him, and he kissed her affectionately and hugged her closer.

'We'll have furniture tomorrow,' he promised, but she wasn't sure she believed him. Tomorrow was a much overused word in the building trade. It normally meant a person would get on to it tomorrow and it might then happen within the next week. If you were lucky. Still, time would tell.

To her amazement, not only were his mother's bits and pieces delivered on Monday but so were the new things which he'd ordered. He'd somehow managed with a combination of bribery and threats to acquire them at zero notice, and the parts of the house that were finished looked lovely. Once pictures were up and curtains hung, the transformation would be amazing, but for now Nick seemed content simply to be able to bring his mother home.

Georgie wondered if she'd see it as home, but, with her things installed and the children around her, perhaps she would.

She came home on Tuesday, the day after the furniture had arrived, and Georgie watched from the site office as he drove her as close as possible to her own entrance at the rear, lifted her into his arms and carried her inside.

Heavens, she looked tiny in his arms. Tiny and frail and broken, like a little bird. There'd be time to go over later, after she'd had time to settle in, and welcome her and ask if there was anything she could do to make the house work better for her, but she was dreading it. What could she say? She hated it, but she remembered when her mother had died, and people ignoring it and avoiding her somehow seemed worse than them talking about it.

So she went, wondering if the woman would even know who she was when she introduced herself, but she needn't have worried. Nick let her in, brushed a quick kiss of welcome over her lips and led her to his mother's sitting room. She was in a chair, her leg with its macabre surgical steel frame raised up on a pretty tapestry footstool, and Nick introduced her.

'Mum, this is Georgie. Georgie, my mother, Liz.'

She summoned a smile. 'Please, come in. You'll have to excuse this hideous contraption. Nick, put the sheet over it so she doesn't have to see it—that's better. So, you're Georgie. I've heard a lot about you,' she said, but then her smile wavered. 'Thank you so much for all your help with the children. Nick tells me you've been working long hours getting the house ready for me, too. I'm really grateful.'

'You're welcome. I'm just so sorry about Lucie,' Georgie said softly. 'If there's anything I can do, anything you need or want to know about the house or the town or anything at all that I can help with, please ask me. Nick knows where to find me, and I've always got my mobile on.'

'She can ask her nurse to call you,' Nick said, and his mother smiled patiently at him and shook her head.

'I've got a broken leg and a broken heart, Nick. There's nothing wrong with my hands or my mouth. If I want to talk to Georgie, I can manage to do it without help.'

'God, Mother, you are so stubborn!' he growled. 'I'm only trying to help—'

'And you are, but I have to do this my way. I have to live with this, Nick. I don't want it suffocating me. Anyway, maybe I won't like your nurse.'

He opened his mouth, shut it and grunted, while Georgie just stood there admiringly and wondered where she'd found so much spirit in the face of such adversity.

'The nurse isn't coming till tomorrow,' he said. 'You'll have to make do with me until then.'

'Heavens. Let's hope we both survive it,' she said, and then, as if she'd realised what she'd said, her face puckered and she turned away.

Time to go, Georgie thought, and went back to her site office. They'd made a huge effort to finish the house in time, and, although it still wasn't completed, they'd switched their energies to the town houses that were being built in the coach house and stable block. It moved the noise away from Liz, and until she was a little stronger, that was how it would stay.

The children came over later in the day, with Una, and moved into their temporary bedroom that night. Una was sleeping in the room beside them with the baby, and Nick was downstairs for now, near his mother.

The Cauldwells' house seemed awfully quiet without them. It should have been peaceful, but it just seemed empty and lonely. She had her own bed back, but it was small consolation. She'd had Harry in bed with her on more than one occasion after he'd woken with a nightmare, and the warm little body snuggled trustingly up to hers had been more than welcome.

Still, if things worked out with her and Nick, they'd see a lot of the children as they were growing up—and she was getting ahead of herself.

'It's just for now,' she told herself sternly. 'Just because he says he loves you doesn't mean he's going to love you forever.'

Even if she'd love him till the day she died.

She stripped the beds, scrubbed the bathroom and vacuumed the house from top to bottom. Or at least she tried. She was on the last stretch of hall carpet when the vacuum cleaner stopped working. She blinked at it, poked the switch, went to the plug to check that it hadn't fallen out and found it in her father's hand.

'What are you doing?' she demanded. 'I want to finish this. Give me the plug, Dad.'

'No, I won't. Stop, Georgie. You've done enough, and you're worn out. Sucking all the life out of the carpets won't change anything.'

She felt her shoulders droop. 'I miss them all,' she said forlornly, and felt her father's arms come round her in a hug.

'Of course you do, but they've only moved down the road. It's not like Jessica and Emily.'

'No, and it won't be,' she said firmly, pushing out of his arms and coiling up the flex. 'They aren't his children, and there's no way they can go back to their poor mother, so it won't arise. I simply won't allow myself to get too attached.'

Her father mumbled something that sounded suspiciously like 'too late for that' and took the cleaner out of her hand, stashed it back in the under-stairs cupboard and shut the door firmly. 'How about a glass of wine?'

'How about a bottle?' she muttered, and wandered into the kitchen aimlessly. What had she done in the evenings before Nick and the children had descended on them? Nothing exciting, but it had filled the time. Now the time seemed to drag, the hands on the clock turning in treacle.

She didn't want wine. She didn't want food.

She wanted Nick, and the children.

The phone rang, and she snatched it off the hook. 'Hello?'

'Georgie?'

'Nick.' She sat on the hard kitchen chair, tucked her heels up to her bottom and hugged her knees to her chest. 'How are things?'

'OK. Mum's exhausted, but she seems to have settled, and the kids are finally out for the count. I just wondered what you were doing.'

'Nothing,' she said with a smile. 'My father confiscated the vacuum cleaner—I was driving him nuts.'

'Missing me?'

'Missing all of you,' she confessed. 'It's awfully quiet.'

'It's quiet here now. I miss you, too. Want to come over and have a drink with me? I've got something to show you.'

'Give me five minutes,' she said and showered rapidly, pulled on jeans and a clean jersey top, found her flip-flops and stuck her head round the door. 'I'm going to see Nick—he's got something to show me in the house,' she said, and, blowing him a kiss, she ran out, jumped in her car and headed over to the house, hoping that it was the speed camera's night off.

He was in the tower. She saw him as she pulled in, and he waved to her and indicated that she should come up.

She let herself in the door at the bottom of the tower and ran lightly up the stairs, looking round in delight as she came up into the room at the top. 'Oh, Nick, it's gorgeous,' she breathed.

The softest leather sofa sat with its back to the wall so it was facing the sea. There was a desk on the other side of it, curving round to the side window, and on the desk was a lamp glowing softly in the late-evening light.

He turned the light off, and the moonlight streamed in through the windows. Taking her hand, he pulled her down onto the sofa, poured two glasses of wine and handed her one, clinking her glass with his.

'To our tower,' he said with a smile, and she clinked her glass on his again and drank to it.

It might only be temporary, but she was going to enjoy every single second of it while it lasted...

Tory came the next day and brought Nick some paperwork to sign and Georgie flowers and a card from Andrew Broomfield.

She opened the card. '"Sorry I gave you such a hard time. Hope your father's improving and that you're finding Nick Barron easier to get answers out of." Well!' She looked up at Nick and laughed. 'Are you easier? That's debatable. I can certainly get answers—but they don't seem to stay the same!'

He chuckled. 'It would be all right if I didn't keep changing the brief. Apparently his wife's OK, by the way, the baby's OK after his operations, and he hasn't lost his house.'

'I wonder why that is?' Tory murmured inno-
cently. 'Couldn't be anything to do with a
hugely magnanimous payout?'

'I got a lot of other properties as part of the deal,
don't forget. The redevelopment opportunities
might be valuable. I'll get you to have a look at
them some time, Georgie. We might be able to do
something there when this place is finished.'

'OK,' she said, letting it sink in. Surely he
wouldn't be talking about the future in that way
if he didn't mean it…?

'And on the subject of this place, are either
of you guys ever going to take me on a guided
tour of the site?' Tory asked, and then turned to
Nick. 'In fact I've chosen my guide. Go and
make us some coffee and talk to your mother.
She was looking a little lost.'

And, linking her arm through Georgie's, she
headed towards the town houses. 'Right, that's
him dealt with. Tell me all about it. How do you
think he is?'

'Nick? Coping, I suppose. He's finding working long-distance difficult and frustrating, but I imagine you're bearing the brunt of that.'

Tory smiled. 'Sorry—not for much longer.'

'You aren't going to Simon!'

'Shh! Not yet. Not until this is all sorted out—and not as his PA. He's asked me to marry him, and we're going to New York.'

'Nick'll be lost without you,' Georgie said, aghast, but Tory just shrugged and smiled ruefully.

'What can I do, Georgie? I love him, and he loves me. When you love someone, you have to compromise. For me, it means giving up a fantastic job with a brilliant boss—brilliant in every sense of the word, by the way—and believe me, that's hard.'

'Does he know yet?'

She shook her head. 'No. That's why I wanted to talk to you. I don't know if I can tell him yet. How's his mother, really?'

Georgie shrugged. 'Improving slowly, I gather, but it's very early days. And her grief will take years to resolve. So will Nick's. If you can give them all a bit longer, I think it would be a kindness.'

Tory nodded. 'OK. I thought that anyway, I just wanted to check with you. Right, now, about this building site. I thought it looked fantastic on plan, but in real life it's even better. These town houses look interesting. Tell me all about them. I might get Simon to buy one so we can come and visit you all.'

All? Oh, please God, but just as it was too soon for Tory to tell him she was leaving, it was too soon for Nick to know how he felt about Georgie, with all the things going on in his life. It might be months before he had time to give their relationship serious consideration, and Georgie could only hope that, by then, their love would have grown to the point that it was strong enough to last, and not shrivelled and dead like the weeds underfoot...

As the days and weeks went on, the site grew closer to completion, and marketing started on the town houses. Nick had pulled the chapel and the sanatorium out of the equation for the time being, for reasons he hadn't really discussed with her, but, as she didn't have time to worry about it, it didn't really matter. There would be plenty of time to deal with those areas later.

They were closer to the house, and she suspected he wanted time to consider their impact on his home now he was actually living there.

And in the meantime, life was good. The weather was fabulous, the kids were a delight and she and Nick managed to sneak many lovely hours alone in their tower.

And their mutual parents, an apparently unlikely combination, were getting on like a house on fire. Liz was much better, the barely tolerated nurse was no longer required, and they'd all grown used to the fixator on her leg. Her father was now driving again, and a couple of times he'd taken Liz out for a little trundle in the car. Georgie was delighted, because apart from anything else it kept her father out of her hair and, more significantly, her site office.

One afternoon in June she was in the site office going over their marketing strategy with Nick when their parents returned from another of their drives.

'The old crocks are back,' Nick murmured, and she dug him in the ribs.

'That's mean. It could be us one day.'

He gave her an odd look. 'Crocked up, or growing old together and coming back from a little drive in the country?'

She shrugged and smiled. 'Either,' she said lightly, but she'd meant the whole growing old together thing. If only, she thought wistfully, but it wasn't likely. She was still waiting for him to wake up and realise that she was just a boring little nobody. It was only a matter of time, she was sure. Once the site was finished and he'd lost interest in the development, then it would all fall apart, and she'd be a fool to tell herself otherwise.

But Nick was giving her funny looks.

'What are you doing tonight?' he asked suddenly.

She shrugged. 'Nothing, particularly. Why?'

'Come to London with me. Una and my mother will be fine with the children, and maybe your father would like to come over and stay here too, to give them a bit of back-up. Archie spends so much time in the house with them all that he'd be quite happy, and the kids would love having him here for a sleepover— what do you say? We can go out for dinner and go to a show and just have some time to ourselves. It's been so long.'

It had. Ages. Apart from stolen moments in

the tower, it had been weeks since they'd been truly alone.

She flashed him a smile. 'Sounds wonderful. I'll start packing!'

'We'd better check with the others first,' he cautioned, but they didn't seem to mind at all. In fact they seemed positively encouraging, so, handing the site keys over to her father, Georgie went home, showered and changed and threw a few things in a case, packed a bag for her father and sorted out some dog food, and then went back to Nick's house.

He opened the door as she walked up the path, his bag standing in the hall behind him and anticipation in his eyes. 'Ready?'

'Absolutely,' she said quietly, unable to stop the smile. 'In fact, forget the show. I'd be quite happy to spend the entire evening in the hot tub. I've been hunched over drawings and specifications for so long now I've got permanent kinks in my spine!'

'I'll give you a back rub,' he promised, his voice a low murmur, and a shiver of anticipation ran through her.

'I'll hold you to that,' she replied, and their eyes locked and burned.

'All set? Right, you two, have a good time and don't worry about this end,' her father said, coming out into the hall behind them. 'If three of us can't keep two small boys and a six-week-old baby under control, it's a pretty poor show. Now go on, off you go and have fun.'

'Are you sure?' she asked, but he was smiling broadly and she had a feeling he was quite looking forward to them being away. There was a flurry of goodbyes, and she slid into Nick's sports car beside him and they set off, the powerful car eating the miles effortlessly.

He turned into the underground car park less than two hours after they'd left, and within moments they were up in his apartment, with the sun still high enough in the sky to feel warm and low enough that it wasn't oppressive.

'Right. I believe you wanted the hot tub,' he said, smiling, and, opening the doors, he pressed the button that lifted the lid away, and turned on the jets with a flourish. 'Your bubbles await.'

They didn't bother with clothes this time. They just stripped off, laughing and racing each other to be the first to slide under the water, and then, legs tangled, eyes meshed, they let their bodies float, supported by the powerful jets that unravelled the kinks in their muscles and left them boneless and utterly relaxed.

The water was cooler than it had been in March, refreshing at the end of a hot day, and Georgie felt all the stresses of the past few weeks melting away. 'I feel wonderful,' she said lazily.

'I noticed,' he replied, sliding one foot up and down the inside of her thigh. 'Absolutely wonderful. Come here.'

And he reached forwards, caught hold of her

hand and reeled her in, so she was lying with her head on his shoulder. 'I promised you a back rub,' he said, and slowly, firmly, his hands started to circle against her spine, holding her closer against his body. Their legs were tangled, her hands were on his shoulders and she could feel the steady beat of his heart under her ear.

'That's gorgeous,' she mumbled, but it wasn't the back rub so much as being in his arms, being alone with him, the luxury of being free to do whatever they wanted. And just then, she wanted to kiss him.

She turned her head, lifted it a fraction and looked up at him. Their mouths were just inches apart, their bodies touching all the way to their toes. And slowly, eyes locked with hers, he brought his head down and touched his lips to hers...

'Oh, that was fabulous. You are so lucky to have a restaurant like that in the building,' she told him, and he laughed and wiped a dribble of strawberry juice from her chin.

Then the laughter faded from his eyes, replaced by something much more intense. 'I love you,' he said softly, and she felt her heart skip as it always did when he said the words. 'You enjoy such simple things, make doing almost anything fun. You've really changed my life—I don't know how I would have got through the last few weeks without you.'

'You would have coped,' she murmured. 'Tory would have helped you, and somehow you would have managed.'

'But not in the same way. I've been able to talk to you in a way I can't talk to anyone else—and we don't even need to talk. I didn't realise how important that was until I had it. You know, it's funny. I didn't think I'd fall in love like this, without warning. I thought it would be a sensible decision, someone who shared the same lifestyle, the same crazy schedules. I thought it would happen gradually, but it didn't. Meeting you was like falling off a cliff. Maybe it's just that for the first time in my life I've met a real woman, and you've knocked me for six.'

She felt the tears prickle her eyes, and reached for his hand. 'Oh, Nick, I love you, too—so much.'

'Enough to marry me?'

For a moment she couldn't believe she'd heard him right, but the look on his face seemed to indicate that he was serious.

She swallowed. 'You want to marry me?'

'If you'll have me.'

She stared at him, looking for the lie in his eyes, but there didn't seem to be one, just love and maybe a little apprehension. Surely he wasn't afraid she'd turn him down?

'Oh, Nick, of course I'll have you,' she said, and then she was in his arms and he was raining kisses down on her face, her eyes, her lips, desperate little kisses that gradually gentled and slowed, resolving into a long, lingering kiss of infinite tenderness.

Then he gathered her to his chest, held her close against his heart and said softly, 'Thank you.'

He held her for an age, then slowly let her go with his right arm, slipping his hand into his pocket and then lifting her left hand in his.

'I don't even know if this'll fit,' he said gruffly, 'but I fell in love with it. It's like you— no frills, just flawless through and through. A perfect diamond.'

She looked down and gasped. 'Oh, Nick,' she breathed, unbearably touched by his words and stunned by the beauty of the simple, delicate ring.

He slid it onto her finger, letting out the breath he was holding when it fitted, and then he lifted her hand to his lips and kissed it.

'I won't be able to wear it for work,' she said, and he smiled.

'I've thought of that. I bought you another diamond, a little drop on a chain to wear round your neck when you can't wear the ring. And anyway, it's not for long. The site'll soon be finished, and then you can wear it every day.'

She turned her hand so that the stone caught the light, and her eyes filled with tears.

'Thank you,' she whispered. 'Oh, Nick, I love you so much.'

And with a little sob she flung her arms round his neck, buried her face in his shoulder and hung on tight.

'Hey! What's this?' He lifted her chin, staring down into her eyes with gentle reprimand. 'Not tonight. We've had enough tears. Come to bed. I want to hold you—and in the morning we'll go home and tell the others.'

'My father will be so pleased. He thinks the world of you.'

'He knows. I've already asked his permission.'

'You've asked—and he didn't let on? The

sneaky old thing! I thought he was grinning like a Cheshire cat!'

Nick laughed. 'Not everyone's like you. Some people can keep a secret.'

She thought of her secret, of Tory's engagement to Simon, and realised that Tory could tell him now. He'd be able to cope with it. He wouldn't be happy, but he'd moved on, putting his sister's death into perspective, and if she was by his side she'd make sure he didn't allow his business life to become too stressful. He'd find another PA. There was probably a good one he could poach from a friend!

'Where will we live?' she asked.

'Here during the week, and Yoxburgh at the weekends, I thought. Depends on my mother's recovery and how good a nanny Una turns out to be. At the moment she's looking good, but you know what they say—the only two things you can be sure of are death and taxes. I won't count my chickens, but I'm sure we'll find a way round it, all of us. The kids won't suffer, I'll make sure of that. If I have to take time out, Tory can manage, but I'll make sure the kids are OK.'

She knew he would. He'd dropped everything to go to them, had almost abandoned his business. If it hadn't been for Tory, she didn't know how he would have held it together in those first days.

'Tory's a star,' she murmured.

'Tory's in love,' he said drily. 'I'm just waiting for her to tell me she's marrying Simon and messing off to the other side of the world.'

She held her breath. Did he know?

'What?'

Rats. Trust him to pick up on it. 'Nothing. I've got cramp in my leg.'

He lifted his head and stared down at her. 'You're a lousy liar. She's doing it, isn't she? Marrying Simon Darcy.' His face broke into a smile, and he reached for the phone.

'Congratulate me,' he said after a moment. 'Georgie's just agreed to marry me.'

There was a little shriek from the other end, and he held the phone away from his ear for a second, and then said into it, 'OK, now it's your turn to confess.'

CHAPTER EIGHT

NEEDLESS to say, their parents were delighted about their engagement. His mother put her slender arms around Georgie and hugged her hard, and when she let her go, there were tears in her eyes.

'I'm so happy for you both,' she said, and Georgie was genuinely touched by her words. She'd gone through so much recently, and she might have resented the intrusion, wanting to keep her son exclusively to herself. But no, she'd welcomed Georgie with open arms, and she felt tears fill her eyes.

'Thank you,' she said, choked, and turned to her father. 'You knew.'

He smiled and opened his arms, wrapping her firmly against his chest and laughing a little emotionally. 'I did. I'm sorry, but that was one secret I had to keep. I'm so happy for you—he's a good man, you deserve him.'

'Does he deserve me, poor man, that's the thing?' she said with a ragged little laugh, and Nick chuckled.

'I'm sure I'll manage to bear it,' he replied. 'Do the kids know?'

'No. That's your job, to tell them,' his mother said with a smile. 'I'm sure they'll be thrilled; they never stop talking about Georgie.'

They *were* thrilled. 'Are you going to be our aunty?' Dickon asked, eyes like saucers, and when she nodded he threw himself into her arms for a hug.

'Harry?'

'Will you and Uncle Nick be in the same bed?' he asked, and she nodded. 'So can I still come in if I have a dream?'

Her eyes filled again. 'Of course you can,' she said, choked, and, reaching out, she drew him into her arms as well. 'You can always come and have a cuddle with me, both of you, at any time. We don't have to be married for that.'

Oh, God, she was going to cry all over them, but then the baby joined in, and Una appeared in the doorway with her, looking unhappy and frustrated. 'I hate to interrupt, but I was just about to go on my day off. Could any of you deal with her?'

'I'll have her,' Nick said, scooping the baby out of her arms and snuggling her close against his shoulder. 'What time will you be back?'

Una shrugged. 'About seven?'

'You can make it later if you like. We'll cope. If you can take over tomorrow morning, that would be good.'

'There's no need. There's nothing for me to do anyway,' she said, and then suddenly burst into tears and ran from the room.

'Oh, hell,' Nick said, scrubbing his hands through his hair and handing the baby to his mother. 'I'll talk to her.'

'I think she's getting homesick,' Liz called after him, and then looked up at them with a worried frown. 'I don't think she's been very happy for the past week or two.'

It seemed she hadn't. Nick came back a few minutes later with the news that Una's boyfriend had given her an ultimatum and wanted her back. 'She's leaving,' he said flatly, and the boys leaned closer to Georgie.

'Does that mean you'll look after us now, Grandma?' Harry asked, and Liz's face puckered.

'Darling, I can't really. My leg—'

'I can help,' George offered. 'We can manage between us most of the time, if you can be around, Nick?'

He gave a heavy sigh and sat down. 'Hobson's choice, really. And Tory's leaving— she's marrying a friend of mine and going to

New York. Boys, how do you feel about going to school?'

Dickon brightened instantly, but Harry leant closer. 'What school?'

'I don't know. I'll have to make enquiries.'

'There's a very good school not far from here,' Georgie told them. 'It's private, and it's probably expensive, but it has a very good reputation for pastoral care as well as academic work, and they take children from three upwards.'

'I'll ring them,' he said. 'If they can take the children now, that gives us a few weeks before the summer holidays to sort something out.'

'What if we don't like it?' Harry asked worriedly.

'Hey, don't think like that,' Georgie said, hugging him. 'I had friends who went to that school, and they loved it there. They had a great time.'

'Have they got a playground?' Dickon asked, and she nodded.

'I believe so.'

'We went to school in Brazil, and I hated it,' Harry said quietly. 'Mummy's boyfriend thought it would be good for us but it wasn't. They were mean.'

'People can be, but it's usually because they aren't very happy themselves,' Georgie told him.

'I'm not mean,' Harry said, pushing out of her arms, and he ran out of the room.

Not happy, but not mean. Oh, poor baby. Georgie looked up at Nick, and he sighed and followed Harry out of the room, calling his name. They were gone for some time, and while they were gone Dickon bombarded Georgie with questions about school until she gave up, laughing. 'I think your Uncle Nick had better phone them and then maybe you can go and have a look.'

'We're going now,' he said, coming back in. 'Harry's coming too, and then we're going for a burger.'

'I thought they were vegetarian,' Georgie murmured, but Nick shrugged.

'Desperate measures. It'll be a chicken burger. They used to have chicken sometimes.'

'We can have chips, anyway,' Dickon said. 'I like chips. Little thin ones. They're tasty. Can we have ketchup?'

Nick met her eyes over the boys' heads. 'Coming with me?'

'To the school? If you like. Dad, can you keep an eye on the site office? There's a delivery of bathroom and kitchen fittings due in some time this morning, for the last of the town houses. Can you get them to put them in the last one?'

'Sure. You go and sort the children out.'

'What about the baby?'

They all looked down at Maya, asleep on her grandmother's knee. 'I can manage her,' Liz said firmly. 'She and I will be all right. If you could just change her nappy and give me a bottle ready, we'll be fine—oh, and the buggy.

I can put her in that and lean on the handle, and we'll cope, won't we, my little one?'

The school was lovely, as Georgie had heard.

Dickon thought the playground was brilliant and wanted to stay in it all morning, but Harry was, as usual, the more reticent.

'They've been through a lot,' Nick explained to the head, while the children were taken off for an informal play session and a snack. 'They lost their mother at the beginning of May, and to be honest I have no idea how much if any schooling they've ever had. They've moved around a lot, had some amazing life experiences, but formal tuition has probably been very slight.'

'They're only young; they'll soon catch up,' the head, Mrs James, said with a smile. She was a kindly woman, but Georgie had no doubt she'd deal with any problems firmly and promptly. If they were her children—which they weren't!—she would have been happy.

'Harry's quite worried,' she said, not sure if Nick would mind her sticking her oar in but doing it anyway.

'I noticed,' Mrs James said. 'He'll cope. We'll keep a very close eye on him. Do you want them to stay for the rest of the day? See how they get on? It might make tomorrow less of a threat. Or you could pick them up after lunch.'

'Ah. We promised them lunch,' Nick said. 'I wouldn't like to break a promise to them.'

'Then just bring them tomorrow. I'm sure they'll be fine.'

'What about uniform?'

'We have a second-hand cupboard. We might be able to find a few things in there to tide you over, or you can go to our suppliers. They're in Woodbridge.'

They foraged in the cupboard first, found a blazer to fit Dickon and shorts and shirts and jumpers for both of them, and that just left a blazer for Harry. 'We'll go and have lunch and then go shopping, shall we?' Nick said, trying to sound enthusiastic, but Harry was unconvinced.

He was a bit happier when he discovered he could have bacon in his chicken burger, and once the blazer was bought and the shoes had been fitted, they went back with a promise of spending the rest of the afternoon on the beach.

'How's she been?' Nick asked his mother worriedly as they went in. She looked exhausted, Georgie thought, and really not very well.

'She's been a good little girl, but I think I might need to see the doctor. My leg's playing up.'

It was. Even Georgie could tell that. It was sore and angry where one of the pins went in, and the trip to the beach had to be abandoned so Nick could take his mother to the hospital. George offered, but he still couldn't really support her weight after his operation, and Nick decided he'd rather do it.

Which left her and her father with two bored

and thwarted children, a grizzly baby and a building site that needed their attention.

If she could just cut herself in half, Georgie thought. Still, the site was just above the beach, the walkie-talkie worked that far, and after checking that they could cope without her for a little while she left her father in charge, rounded up the troops and they set off for the beach, with Archie glued to Harry's side.

They built a fort, and Archie dug the moat, and the baby slept peacefully for an hour. It was too good to be true, she thought, and then Nick appeared.

'Uncle Nick! Come and help us build the fort!' Dickon said excitedly, and grabbed his hand, but he shook his head.

'Sorry, Dickon, I can't. I have to go back to the hospital. They want Grandma to stay in, because her leg's a bit sore,' Nick explained. 'I'll come and see it, though. Let me just talk to Georgie for a minute.'

She stood up, brushing the sand off her legs, and they moved away a little.

'What's wrong?' she asked worriedly.

He sighed and scrubbed his hand through his hair. 'She's got a pin track infection, apparently, and they want to do scans and things to see if they can take the frame off yet. She's on an antibiotic drip for the night.'

'Oh, no. Nick, I'm sorry.'

'So am I. I really need to get back to London, and without her here I just can't do that.'

'Una will be back tonight. Can't you ask her if she can stay another week or two?'

'I can ask, but it'll probably be no. I wonder if I can get someone else.'

'Ask Tory.'

He snorted. 'Tory's busy planning her escape.'

'Rubbish. She'll sort you, Nick. Just ask her.'

'And in the meantime? I have to take the children to school tomorrow, I know that, but then what? If I run down to London and don't get back, who'll pick up the kids? Una can't drive, if she's even still here, and if you do it then your father's taking on too much on the site.'

'Nonsense. He's in his element, but there are things he's not up to speed on, changes that you've made that might not be written down. It's not a physical problem, it's a factual one— and the fact is, I need to be on site. He can get the boys from school, though, if you really can't get back. I think you should, though. It's their first day, Nick. It's important.'

'It's all important,' he growled. 'And what about the baby?'

Georgie shrugged. 'You could take her to London with you? At least you'll know where she is.'

'Yeah—I'll be able to hear her screaming! Oh, God, this is such a mess. I could kill Una.'

'You don't mean that.'

He sighed. 'No, of course I don't. Damn. We'll sort it out tomorrow. I have to take

Mum some things. Want me to give you a hand to get back to the house before the little one kicks up?'

And right on queue, she started to grizzle.

Georgie gave a frustrated smile. 'You spoke too soon.'

It went downhill. Una wanted to go the next day, and so Nick ordered a taxi to take her to the airport.

His mother's scan results were not good, and she was told she'd have to stay in for several days. Against her better judgement Nick had had her moved to the private wing, and it made it easier to take the children in to see her that evening.

'So, are you looking forward to school in the morning?' she asked brightly, and Dickon beamed, but Harry's face was shuttered and withdrawn, and Georgie worried for him.

She was on site at seven in the morning, but there was no sign of Nick. He always came out to see her, but today, she guessed, he was up to his eyes with the boys.

Oh, well, she didn't have time to worry about them. She had her own problems. Her father had done his best, but, because she'd tried to keep the load off him, she hadn't involved him in all the little changes. And he'd made a couple of mistakes which now had to be rectified.

A lorry arrived with a delivery, and the digger was parked right where she wanted the driveway blocks unloaded. No sign of the digger driver, but the key was on the hook, so she went out, ignoring the ringing phone, and climbed up into the cab, firing up the engine.

As she started to lift the bucket she saw a flash of colour out of the corner of her eye, but when she looked up there was nothing. Shrugging, she eased the lever and raised the bucket up, just as the cab door flew open and Nick wrenched her hand off the lever.

'Stop!' he yelled, his face panic-stricken. 'Dickon's in the bucket!'

'What?' She leapt out and ran round, to see Harry sitting on the ground crying and Dickon peering white-faced out of the bucket overhead.

'Stay there,' she told him firmly. 'Don't move a muscle. Harry, move back a little further, darling. Nick, lift him down the moment the bucket's in reach.'

And, trembling, her legs like jelly, she climbed back up into the digger, lowered the bucket until it was level with Nick and then waited while he snatched the child to safety before backing it out of the way, parking it up and running over to them.

'They didn't want to go to school,' Nick said, his face agonised.

'I did,' Dickon piped up. 'It was Harry's idea to hide. I thought the digger would be a fun place to go. I didn't know you were going to move it. Harry jumped out, but I was too scared…' And his little chin started to wobble.

Georgie didn't care. She'd nearly killed them both, and she could have done it then with her bare hands. Or the person who was supposed to be in charge.

She turned to Nick, ignoring his pale face and agonised expression, and tore into him.

'What the hell did you think you were doing, letting them come on the site? I know you don't take site safety seriously, but they could have been *killed,* Nick! Don't you think your family's gone through enough?'

He recoiled as if she'd slapped him, then, taking Harry by the hand, he turned on his heel and marched them back to the house without a word.

'So where do you want these blocks, love?'

'Over there—and don't call me love!' Georgie snapped, and stalked back into the site office, slammed the door and burst into tears.

Ten minutes later she saw the estate car

leaving, the two boys in the back and Nick grim-faced behind the wheel. She wondered where the baby was, and decided it wasn't her problem. He could manage the baby. He could manage all of them.

Then Una appeared in the doorway in tears. 'I never wanted the boys to be hurt. I should have been watching them, but I was packing. Nick was bathing the baby—Georgie, I'm so sorry.'

Oh, lord. Not Nick's fault at all, then, but Una's. 'Where's the baby now?'

'With Nick. He's going to London. The taxi is coming to get me. Georgie, I'm so sorry—for all of it. For leaving, and making it this bad thing between you and Nick.'

Georgie sighed. 'It's OK,' she relented, and hugged Una. 'I hope your boyfriend's pleased to see you. Good luck.'

'Thank you. Oh—my taxi. I must go. Say goodbye to the boys for me.'

'I will. Safe journey.'

She watched her go with a sinking heart. She'd been good to the children, and without her their lives would all be vastly more complicated.

No. Nick's life would be, and his mother's. Hers wasn't involved. They weren't his children. It was temporary. He just needed to get another nanny to care for the children while Liz got better, and it would all sort itself out.

It had to.

It was a hellish day. The baby screamed, Tory announced she was leaving in three weeks and there wasn't a nanny available till Monday, at least.

'I'll pay twice as much,' he said to Tory, but the agency weren't interested.

'It isn't about money,' Tory said. 'I've already offered them three times the going rate. They just don't have anyone reliable until Monday, so you'll just have to cope. What's going to happen if you don't come to work, Nick? You might lose a few hundred thousand here and there. You can afford it. Your family's more important.'

She was absolutely right, of course.

'Monday, then,' he growled. 'And she'd better be fantastic.'

The only high point in the day was his phone call to the school, which revealed that the boys had settled in fine and were having a great time. He wasn't sure he believed it, but he'd interrogate them once he got home and find out just how great it had really been. Until then he'd have to take Mrs James on trust.

And in the meantime, he had work to do— shedloads of it, if his business wasn't going to go completely down the pan.

Frankly, he wasn't sure he cared.

Nick's apology was short and to the point. He came onto the site just as she was locking up, his face stiff with strain and emotion, and his voice was carefully controlled.

'I'm sorry. I wasn't looking after them at the time, but that doesn't excuse me. You were right, they're my responsibility and they could have been killed. It won't happen again.'

And he walked off. No hug, no sorry, I'm an idiot, forgive me. Just my fault, it won't happen again. And he looked exhausted. She would have followed him, but the set of his shoulders was pretty unwelcoming.

Oh, damn. She felt the tears prickle her eyes, and blinked hard. This was so stupid. He'd obviously had a hell of a day, she wanted to know how the children had got on at school, he would need to visit his mother in hospital and if she didn't unbend, a difficult day was just going to be even worse.

'Nick?'

He stopped and turned. 'What?'

'I'm sorry.'

He came back to her, unsmiling, and stopped a foot away.

'What for?'

She shrugged. 'I yelled at you in front of them. I shouldn't have done that, but I just felt sick. I could have killed them. I should have checked the bucket before I got in the digger. It isn't only your fault, or Una's, and it certainly isn't the boys'.'

His face softened, and he reached for her. 'Come here. I've had a hell of a day. The last thing I need is to fight with you.'

She slid her arms round him and hugged him tight, and he rested his chin on her head and sighed.

'How did the boys get on?'

'OK, I think. Not nearly as bad as Harry had thought, and he seems to have made a friend. Dickon thought it was great.'

She smiled against his shirt and lifted her head. 'Want a babysitter tonight so you can see your mother?'

He searched her eyes. 'Are you sure?'

'What else am I going to do?'

He laughed without humour. 'Run away with me?'

'Don't tempt me. Look, I'm all hot and sticky and dusty. Let me go home and shower and change, and I'll come back. You can see your mother, I'll feed the kids and maybe we can get a takeaway later.'

'What about your father?'

'Unless I'm very much mistaken, he'll make himself a sandwich and settle down in front of the television for the night. He saw your mother this afternoon, and he's been helping out here, and I think he's ready for an early night. So, shall we do that?'

'Sounds good.' He kissed her lingeringly. 'See you later. Don't be long.'

She wasn't, and by the time he came back from visiting his mother, takeaway in hand, the boys were tucked up in bed, fast asleep, the baby was just finishing her bottle and Georgie was ready to put her feet up. Big time.

She burped the baby, settled her in her cot and went through to the kitchen. He'd found the warmed plates and opened the cartons, and she sniffed appreciatively and stuck her finger in the curry sauce. 'Yum. I'm glad I'm marrying you. You do good food.'

'I do good all sorts of things,' he said with a grin. 'I got passanda and dansak. Didn't know what you'd like—and there's a peshwari naan and pilau rice.' He brandished a bottle of wine at her, and she blew him a kiss.

'You little star,' she said, and he grinned.

'You look ready for it.'

'You, too. Has it been a killer day?'

'Awful. I want to talk to you about it. Let's eat first.'

'I'm not going back to London.'

She sat bolt upright on the little sofa in the tower room and stared at him. 'What? Never?'

'Not for ages. I need to be more involved

with the children. There's a nanny starting on Monday, and Tory's in the office another three weeks. That should give me time to decide what I want to do with my life, but it can't go on like it has for the last few years, and I don't want it to. It's just working out what to do instead that's difficult.'

She tipped her head on one side and studied him thoughtfully. 'Tell me to mind my own business if you like, but do you actually need to work?'

He gave a wry laugh. 'Only to stop myself going crazy. Not for money, no.'

'So if you were careful, you wouldn't have to work again?'

He chuckled and pulled her closer. 'I don't even need to be that careful. The only reason I'm working is because I have to do something with my life, and because there are a lot of people out there who benefit from the business. We sponsor a lot of charities, support individual ventures, that sort of thing. So, no, I don't need to work, but I should, and I wouldn't want to stop that side of it.'

She should have known. Should have worked it out, because he was too kind to keep it all to himself. And despite the car and the hot tub, he didn't surround himself in luxury. The house, for instance—the spec was high, but nothing extraordinary, nothing outrageous or ostentatious. He just wasn't like that, and it was part of the reason she loved him.

'How about property development?' she suggested. 'You've got quite an interesting portfolio already, with the apartment in London, this site here and all Andrew Broomfield's shop units. And you could run that from anywhere.'

'Mmm. And you could be the resident architect. If we converted the chapel, it would provide office space and a design studio for you…'

She swivelled round and looked searchingly at him. 'You've thought all this through, haven't you?'

'Some of it. Just a few ideas. I haven't made any decisions. Would you be interested?'

She snuggled back. 'Could be. I'm more interested in getting this site done and dusted at the moment, but in the future—yes, maybe.'

He pressed his lips to the top of her head and sighed. 'Want to stay the night?'

She laughed softly. 'I'd love to, but we aren't married. What about the children?'

'Hmm. You're right. We'll just have to get married nice and soon, and then I can have you to myself all night.'

She could hardly wait.

The next few days were hectic on the site, but Nick was around and he and the boys waved to her from the other side of the site fence on their way to and from the beach. Goodness knew when he was working—all night, probably, in between feeding the baby and doing the washing.

She saw him every evening, but the mornings were too busy and she longed for Sunday. They were working on Saturday to get the site ready for marketing; the carpet was being laid in the show house on Monday, and the landscapers were due to start, so she'd put a crew to work clearing around the houses and they were hard at work on the gardens. By the time they'd finished, Nick was visiting his mother, and she went home and found her father was also out.

Never mind. She was too tired to speak, so she simply had a bath and fell into bed without bothering to eat. Her father woke her at nine in the morning with a cup of tea, and sat on the edge of her bed.

'How are you? You look worn out.'

'I am. Busy day yesterday clearing the site ready for the landscapers. It's looking great, though.'

'It is. I'm proud of you. You've pulled this all together really well, and I can't tell you how thrilled I am about you and Nick. It's such good news about the children—you must be really happy.'

'The children?'

'Mmm. I think it's wonderful. You'll be a real family. Liz is so relieved, because this leg of hers is going to take ages to heal, and she's been so worried, but now you're going to adopt them, she won't have to worry at all.'

Georgie stared at him, stunned. 'Adopt them?' she said blankly. 'We aren't going to adopt them. She's going to look after them, with the new nanny who starts on Monday. Nick and I are going to help at the weekends.'

Her father looked just as puzzled. 'But…Liz said Nick had told her—he must have discussed it with you, surely?'

'No, he hasn't,' she said, throwing back the covers, 'but trust me, he will.'

She grabbed her clothes, went into the bathroom and scrubbed her teeth, yanked on her clothes and stormed out. What the hell was he thinking about? Sure, it was a fantastic idea to adopt the kids. The best possible thing for them—but when had he decided to do it? Yesterday? The day before? Or weeks ago, when getting a nanny had proved to be so darned hard? How long had the idea been in his mind?

Since before he'd told her he loved her? Dammit, he'd asked her to marry him, and she'd thought it was because he really loved her, but what if it wasn't? What if it was just an easy way to get a nanny on tap, and all his professions of love were just pretty lies?

Her heart breaking, she skidded to a halt outside his house, went in without knocking and ran up to the tower room. He was sitting at the desk, the children nowhere to be seen, and he lifted his head and started to smile. Then he must have registered her face, and he shut the top of his laptop and stood up.

'Georgie?'

She straightened up, lifted her chin and glared at him.

'When were you going to tell me?'

CHAPTER NINE

NICK stared at her in confusion.

'When was I going to tell you what?'

'That you're adopting the children.'

His brow pleated, then he closed his eyes and sat down on the edge of his desk with a sigh. 'It was only an idea—'

'The way my father told it, it sounded like more than just an idea—it sounded like a *fait accompli.*'

He sighed harshly and rammed his hands through his hair. 'Nonsense. But my mother can't cope, and what other choice is there? I'm giving up my business, for heaven's sake! Throwing away everything I've worked for and moving up here because I have to, Georgie. I didn't ask for any of this. I don't need a couple of little tearaways and a screaming baby chucked into the middle of my life, but I'm dealing with it, because the kids need a responsible, capable adult, and that means me. For God's sake, be reasonable—'

'What? You've suddenly introduced three other people into the equation and you're telling me to be *reasonable?* Didn't it occur to you to discuss it with me?'

'I was going to—'

'When? After we were married? And that's convenient, isn't it? You've just met me, you know I'm single, we're getting on OK and suddenly, bang, you inherit a few kids and they need a mother. Oh, how handy, here's Georgie, but we'd better not tell her, we'll just lure her with a few lies and a pretty bauble—'

She wrenched the ring off and hurled it at him, then her hand went up to her neck and she yanked at the necklace, but the chain was too strong and she couldn't break it, and it hurt her neck, and she felt the hot, bitter tears scald her eyes.

'You're a bastard, do you know that? Just like Martin. You didn't want me at all, you just wanted a free resident nanny for the children, and there I was, like a sitting duck. What was it you said to Tory? Don't listen to Simon, it's all lies. Were you speaking personally, Nick? Judging him by your own standards? And such pretty lies. All that rubbish about loving me, about me being like the diamond—'

She yanked again, and the chain flew apart in her hands, the diamond pinging against the window and falling unheeded to the carpet.

Wordlessly he stared at her, then bent and picked up the ring and slipped it into his shirt pocket, his face expressionless.

'If that's what you really think of me, then there's nothing more to say, is there?' he said tightly. 'I thought you loved me. I thought you loved the kids, but I was wrong, you don't want to be bothered with them at all. You've done everything you can to keep your distance, to avoid them. Like all the others, you were just after what you could get from me. Only the other day you were asking what I was worth—'

'I didn't! I asked if you needed to work, if you could afford the luxury of giving up your company and moving up here. I don't want your damned money! It hasn't exactly made you happy, has it?'

'Apparently not,' he said. 'But one thing I'm sure of—you aren't getting it. I'll save it for the people who deserve it. Now, if you've got nothing else to say, perhaps you'd better leave.'

She opened her mouth, thought better of it and turned on her heel. As she did so she heard a door slam far below her, and, looking up, she saw Harry running down the drive, with Dickon struggling to keep up. As she watched they ran out of the gate and down the road towards the beach.

'Where are they going?' she asked in horror, and Nick stared out, swore softly and pushed her aside, throwing himself down the stairs after them.

They must have heard, she thought in horror. Must have heard Nick say she didn't love them. With a choking sob she fled after him, ran out of the door at the bottom of the tower and sprinted down over the lawn. Nick had followed the children out of the gate, but the wall was quicker, and she swung her legs over and slithered down it, dropping the last few feet and racing across the road.

'They must be going round the point,' she yelled to him, heading off across the sand, and then he was beside her, calling the children, scrambling after them over the rocks. She followed him, her feet slipping in her haste, and as she straightened up a wave caught her foot and she stared down in dismay.

The tide was coming in, and if they went much further they'd be cut off.

'Nick, the tide!' she yelled, and he nodded grimly.

'I know. How long have we got?'

'Five minutes?'

He swore and set off again, just a few feet in front of her. They were gaining on the boys, and if only they'd stop it would be all right, but Dickon had his hands over his ears and Harry turned and yelled, 'Go away! You don't want us! Leave us alone!'

She bit back a sob and pulled off her shoes. She was faster without them, her foothold more certain, and she overtook Nick and caught up with them just as the tide reached them.

'Come on, boys,' she said desperately, holding out her hands. 'Please come back. We do want you. We both want you. We love you to bits.'

'So why were you shouting all those things?' Harry asked accusingly. 'You said Nick didn't love you, and he said why would he want two tearaways and a screaming baby—'

'We both said all sorts of things,' Nick said, coming up beside her, his face tortured. 'Stupid things. Things we need to talk about some more, but not here and not now. Boys, the tide's coming in. We have to go back now. Really. We can talk about it inside.'

He reached for Harry, but the boy pulled his hand away and shoved his arms behind his back defiantly. 'You don't love me,' he said accusingly, then he turned on Georgie. 'You said I could sleep in your bed if I wanted, but you aren't even in our house and Uncle Nick's not the same, and you promised—'

'But we aren't married yet.'

'Mummy wasn't married to Dom. They used to sleep in the same bed. People do if they love each other, he said, but you don't, so you can't love each other and you don't love us, and we just want Mummy back.'

And his lip wobbled, and Dickon started to cry, and Georgie bit her lip so hard it bled.

'Oh, Harry,' Nick said unevenly. 'If I could give you back your mother, I would—and not because I don't want you. I love you—I've always loved you, you know that. I'm sorry I said those things. It wasn't fair. Please—come on.' He held out his hand, and for an age Harry stood there, then slowly, great tears rolling down his face, he reached out his hand and put it in Nick's.

'Thank God,' he said, scooping the boy up into his arms and hugging him fiercely. 'Georgie, bring Dickon,' he snapped, and she lifted the little boy into her arms and wiped the tears from his face.

'I'm so sorry,' she said, hugging him, and his little arms slipped round her neck and he snuggled closer. She turned to go back, and gasped as a wave broke over her foot. The rocks were piled against the foot of the old sea wall, and where they were standing was a high point. The way back was now completely cut off, and the way forward was worse.

She tried to remember what time high tide was, and realised there was still an hour to go. And in an hour they'd be up to their waists, and with the current they'd be swept off the rocks and washed out to sea.

She looked up at the wall, and Nick caught her eyes and shook his head.

'No way. We can't do it. We'll have to go back the way we came.'

'We can't. It's too deep already. Nick, I can do it. I can get up there and lift the kids to safety. If it wasn't for the fence, I could run for a rope from the site and bring it back, but I can at least get us all up there.'

'Not me. Georgie, you can't get me up there.'

'I can try—'

He shook his head. 'I can't do it. I've tried before. I'll hand you up the kids and you can stay with them while I go back round. I'm strong enough to make it if we hurry, but we haven't got long.'

Not long at all, she realised as the water hit the wall and soaked her to mid-thigh. Dickon sobbed and wriggled closer, and she prised his arms away from her neck and handed him to Nick.

'I'll go up as far as I can, then hand me Dickon first,' she said. She studied the wall for a moment, moved along a little and picked her way carefully up it. It wasn't the easiest place, because the concrete here was smoother and there were fewer hand-holds, but finally she found a spot high enough up the wall, where she could get a purchase with both feet and jam her fingers into a crack big enough to hold her weight.

'Right, pass me Dickon,' she said, reaching down with her free hand and grabbing a handful of his T-shirt as Nick held him aloft. She pulled him up to her chest, kissed him and hugged him, then, pinning him against the wall with her body, she got a better grip, hoisted him up onto her shoulder and pushed him over the edge onto the top of the wall.

'OK?'

'OK,' he said tremulously.

She threw him a smile. 'Good boy. Now stay there, and sit very, very still, and I'll get Harry, OK?'

He nodded, and she reached back down to repeat the procedure. It was much harder. Nick was able to lift him higher because he had both arms free this time, but Harry was heavier than his brother, and Georgie's fingers were starting to ache, and it was all she could do to hold his weight.

'I need a better hold,' she said, and let go, grasped his T-shirt again and hauled with the last of her strength.

His wiry little arms closed round her, he burrowed into her side and she leant against the wall, trapping him in comparative safety while she got her breath back.

'Right, Harry, climb up me,' she said, but he wouldn't let go, and then she heard Nick say her name and turned to see the waves creaming around his knees.

'I have to go,' he said softly. 'I'll be as quick as I can. Just stay there with him like that. He's too heavy for you to struggle with, and we can't waste any time.'

She felt his hand squeeze her leg, then he was gone, heading back over the rocks in the swirling water, feeling his way blindly over the submerged rocks as the surging sea tugged at him.

'Please, God,' she whispered, but she couldn't go on. She couldn't voice her fears, not in front of the children and maybe not even to herself. If the waves caught him...

She looked up and smiled at Dickon reassuringly, and then looked back to Nick. His progress was painfully slow, but he had made it through the low section and was now travelling faster over another high section like the one immediately below her. Not that it seemed very high. The rocks were gone, nothing but the sea breaking right below her feet and splashing her legs.

He started to go down again, and was almost out of sight around the corner when a wave came, bigger than all the rest. She saw him stagger, arms waving as he lost his balance, and then he disappeared from view. Her heart jammed in her throat. Where was he? Was he gone, dragged into the swirling water amongst the rocks?

He'll be smashed to bits, she thought, staring in horror at the spot where he'd been standing. Oh, God, she shouldn't have let him go. She should have made him try to climb the wall, he could have done it if she'd made him, but she hadn't, and now he'd been swept out to sea.

'Where's Uncle Nick?' Dickon asked, his voice panicking. 'I can't see him any more.'

'He's gone round the corner,' she said, trying

to inject some confidence into her voice. 'He'll be back with help in a minute.'

'I'm scared,' Harry mumbled against her shoulder. His little body was shaking, and she tightened her hold on him and pressed a kiss to his head.

'We'll be fine,' she said cheerfully. 'He'll be here just any minute.'

But it wasn't minutes, it was ages, and still he didn't come, and the sea was crashing over her legs and threatening to dislodge her. She lost the toe-hold of her right foot for a moment, her toes so cold she couldn't feel the way back in, just had to keep trying until her foot seemed able to bear weight again, relieving the strain on her left hand and foot.

'Hold tight,' she said, and, letting go of Harry, she found another hold with her right hand, so she was spread-eagled on the face of the wall with him clamped firmly onto her and pressed into the concrete face.

She rested her cheek against the rough surface and closed her eyes. Please let him be all right, she thought. Don't let him die. Not like this, with all those awful words between us. And it was Sunday. Her father knew she'd gone to talk to Nick, and wouldn't call her. There was nobody due on site, his mother was in hospital, and there was nobody who'd miss any of them and raise the alarm.

If he didn't come soon, if, God forbid, he'd been washed out to sea and drowned, then the waves would dislodge her and she and Harry would fall into the water, and poor Dickon would be stuck there, alone and terrified, and Maya was in the house by herself, probably hungry and thirsty and with no one to go to her—

'Hello? Is there anybody there?'

'Help!' she yelled, and then they were there, big, strong men from the coastguards, cutting through the wire fence and lifting

Dickon to safety, reaching down for Harry, then pulling her up…

'Where's Nick?' she said, her fear for him rising up to choke her, but then she heard his voice and relief made her weak.

'I'm here,' he said, straightening up with Dickon in one arm and Harry wrapped around his legs. His other arm was hanging at a strange angle, and blood was streaming down his face from a cut on his brow, but he was alive, and so were the children.

'So what kept you?' she said, but her smile wobbled and she bit her lip, the tears falling anyway, and she took him gently in her arms and hugged him.

He was soaked and frozen, his body was shaking like a leaf and he was covered in blood, but he was the best thing she'd seen in her entire life, and she couldn't take her eyes off him.

'I thought—'

'I know. So did I,' he said, and bent and

kissed her as if his life depended on it. Maybe it did. She knew hers did.

'Come on, mate, let's get you lot to hospital and sort you out,' a coastguard said. One of them took Dickon, another took Harry, and for a moment she wondered if they'd pick her up, too, but Nick put his arm round her—his good arm, because the other one was obviously badly injured—and together they straggled back through the garden of the house above the point and up to the waiting ambulance.

'What about Maya?' she said, remembering the baby suddenly.

'Who's Maya?' the ambulance driver said.

'The baby. She's in that house over there,' Nick said, pointing.

'I'll get her,' Georgie said, but the paramedic stopped her.

'You've got bare, bleeding feet, your fingers are in shreds. You're going nowhere. Just tell them how to get in and where to go.'

So she gave them directions while they im-mobilised Nick's arm and taped gauze over her fingers and toes, and the driver and one of the coastguards went to fetch the baby while they checked over the children.

'We'll have to call another ambulance,' the paramedic said, but Georgie shook her head and the children huddled up to her.

'We're going together or not at all,' Nick said flatly, and after a token protest the paramedic shrugged and smiled.

'Just don't tell the boss,' she said, and then, loading everyone up, they set off for the hospital, the baby strapped to the front seat in her baby seat, Georgie sitting between the children in the back, Nick's good hand hanging on to her bandaged fingers as if he'd never let her go, and frankly it couldn't have been tight enough.

'I love you,' he said, and she knew she was crying but she didn't care, because she'd thought she'd never hear him say those words again.

'I love you, too—and I'm so sorry I threw the ring at you. I didn't mean it. I was just angry that you hadn't talked to me, but when I thought I'd lost you—'

'Shh. It doesn't matter now. We'll talk later,' he said.

He closed his eyes, his face taut with pain, but his fingers didn't slacken their grip until they arrived at the hospital and unloaded him.

Then he was whisked away, and she had to register them all.

'So are you his wife?' the nurse asked.

'No—but I soon will be,' she said firmly, crossing her bandaged fingers.

'And are these your children or his?'

'Ours,' she said.

'Our mummy's dead,' Dickon told her. 'Uncle Nick and Georgie are going to look after us. I think,' he added, and Georgie hugged him, hating herself for making him doubt their love.

'Uncle Nick and Georgie are definitely going

to look after you,' she promised. 'We're adopting them,' she told the nurse. 'And their grand-mother's here in hospital at the moment. She was injured in the accident that killed their mother.'

'Oh, dear. You are in the wars,' the nurse said gently, and got a doctor who checked them over again thoroughly, while the nurse phoned her father and asked him to come in.

'They're fine, if a little shocked,' the doctor said, and looked at her fingers and toes. 'These just need cleaning and dressing, and then you can go,' he told her, and the nurse wrapped them in neat little tubes.

'Your father's on his way,' she said. 'He sounded a bit worried, so I tried to reassure him, but I don't think he'll be happy till he's seen you.'

'I can imagine. Any news of Nick?' she asked worriedly, and the nurse smiled and patted her hand comfortingly.

'I'll go and find out. Stay here.'

She was back minutes later. 'He's dislocated

his shoulder,' they were told. 'They're going to put it back in under sedation, and then he can go home once it's been strapped up.'

Just then there was a yelp, and a sob of relief, and she met the nurse's eyes. 'That was him,' she said, her heart hammering at the thought of him in pain.

'Sounds like it's back. Hang on, I'll see if you can go and sit with him.'

She came back with a smile, and led them through to Nick. He was lying propped up, his arm now in the right place resting on his chest, the cut on his head held together with little white strips, and he greeted them with a tired smile.

'Hi there,' he said, sounding slurred. 'You all OK?'

'We're fine,' she said, and the children huddled closer.

'Are you going to die?' Harry said, and he shook his head as if to clear it, sat up and bent over, pressing a kiss to Harry's head.

'No, Harry, I'm not going to die. I have far too much to do—starting with convincing Georgie that I really do want to marry her.'

'Job done,' she said, her eyes filling. 'You aren't getting rid of me that easily.'

'Thank God for that,' he said, and lay back and closed his eyes.

'Right, we need to strap him up, and then you can take him home,' the doctor said cheerfully, and Georgie and the children trooped out, the baby seat hanging from Georgie's battered fingers, and met her father in the corridor.

His face creased with emotion, and he gathered them all into his arms and hugged them fiercely. 'How is he?'

'He's going to be fine,' she said, and then burst into tears.

'Are you OK?'

Nick's eyes fluttered open and he held out his

good arm to her, gathering her against his chest. 'I'm fine. How are the kids?'

'OK. They're sleeping. They're both in Harry's bed, and the baby's in their room with them. I've fed and changed her and she's settled down. Are you really OK?'

'Bit sore, but better than it was. Georgie, I've got something to tell you.'

She sat up and stared down at him, fear clawing through her. 'Sounds serious,' she said, trying for a light note and not feeling in the least bit light.

'I've lost the ring—you threw it at me and I put it in my pocket and now it's gone, washed away. I've lost it. I'm so sorry.'

'Is that all? Oh, God, Nick, I thought you were going to tell me you didn't love me, didn't want me…'

His arm tightened, hauling her down against his chest. 'No way. When that wave caught me and dragged me under, all I could think was that

I was going to die and nobody would help you, and you'd be washed away, and Dickon would be sitting there on the wall alone—'

'And the baby was in the house with nobody to hear her—I know,' she said. 'I went through it all. And all I could think was that you'd died thinking I didn't love you. The ring doesn't matter, it's just a ring, but if I'd lost you—'

'Come to bed,' he said hoarsely. 'I need to hold you—need to talk to you about the children.'

So she slipped off her clothes and snuggled into bed beside him in her underwear, and he wrapped his arm round her. 'I'm so sorry you found out like that about the adoption thing,' he said, 'but I promise you, I didn't mean to spring anything on you. It was only an idea. Mum was worried sick, her leg's going to take ages to heal because she's got an infection in the bone, apparently, and I couldn't see a better way. I said it really to reassure her, and it wouldn't affect who the children lived with, but as soon as I said it it seemed such a good idea, so simple and obvious I couldn't believe I hadn't thought of it before. I never dreamt you'd think I'd cooked up our whole relationship to trap you. I still can't believe you'd think it of me.'

'I don't. I didn't, not really, that's why I was so shocked, but when Martin's wife became ill and he ended up with the children, he suddenly decided he was in love with me and wanted to marry me. And they were so sweet, the same age as Harry and Dickon, and then his wife got better and he got us all together and told us that she wanted the children back, and so they'd be going back to her. They were delighted, of course, because they missed her, but then he said I wouldn't be there any more and they wouldn't see me, and—oh, Nick, I'll never forget the look in their eyes. They thought I'd betrayed them, and I was devastated. And then when our relationship was just beginning to go somewhere,

Lucie died and you had the children. And then you told me you loved me, and out of nowhere you asked me to marry you just when Una decided she couldn't stay any longer, and then Dad said you wanted to adopt them—'

'And it all seemed to fit. Except it doesn't, you know. Get my wallet.'

'What?'

'My wallet—it's on the chest of drawers there.'

She slipped out of bed and picked it up, bringing it back to the bed and handing it to him.

'Open it—look in the zipped bit at the back. There's a receipt.'

'This one?' she asked, mystified, and handed it to him.

'That's the one. Open it.'

She unfolded the sheet of paper and stared at it. 'It's the ring and necklace—my God! Nick, the price of it!'

'Forget the price of it. Look at the date, Georgie.'

'April.' She looked up at him. 'You bought it in April.'

'Before Lucie died. I was going to propose to you the weekend of Simon's party, but I'd forgotten about the party and so I was going to do it over breakfast on Sunday morning.'

'Only Lucie went into labour.'

'And everything fell apart.'

She dropped the receipt and closed her eyes. 'Oh, Nick, I could have lost you. I so nearly did, and all because I didn't dare to believe you could really love me.'

'Oh, I love you. I've loved you since you ripped my head off for not checking into the site office. I've loved you since you howled your eyes out because I'd cleared your debts and then took me out for breakfast at lunchtime. And I don't intend to stop loving you.'

'Thank goodness for that,' she said, sliding back into bed beside him, 'because you're going to be stuck with me for the rest of your life, and it'll make it a lot more fun if you love me back.'

He chuckled ruefully and hugged her closer.

'I like the sound of that,' he said, and, pressing his lips to her hair, he sighed softly and fell asleep…

MILLS & BOON® PUBLISH EIGHT LARGE PRINT TITLES A MONTH. THESE ARE THE EIGHT TITLES FOR MARCH 2007

❦

PURCHASED FOR REVENGE
Julia James

THE PLAYBOY BOSS'S CHOSEN BRIDE
Emma Darcy

HOLLYWOOD HUSBAND, CONTRACT WIFE
Jane Porter

BEDDED BY THE DESERT KING
Susan Stephens

HER CHRISTMAS WEDDING WISH
Judy Christenberry

MARRIED UNDER THE MISTLETOE
Linda Goodnight

SNOWBOUND REUNION
Barbara McMahon

THE TYCOON'S INSTANT FAMILY
Caroline Anderson

MILLS & BOON®

Live the emotion

0207 Rom LP

MILLS & BOON® PUBLISH EIGHT LARGE PRINT TITLES A MONTH. THESE ARE THE EIGHT TITLES FOR APRIL 2007

———————— ❧ ————————

THE CHRISTMAS BRIDE
Penny Jordan

RELUCTANT MISTRESS, BLACKMAILED WIFE
Lynne Graham

AT THE GREEK TYCOON'S PLEASURE
Cathy Williams

THE VIRGIN'S PRICE
Melanie Milburne

THE BRIDE OF MONTEFALCO
Rebecca Winters

CRAZY ABOUT THE BOSS
Teresa Southwick

CLAIMING THE CATTLEMAN'S HEART
Barbara Hannay

BLIND-DATE MARRIAGE
Fiona Harper

MILLS & BOON®

Live the emotion

0307 Rom LP